DAY AFTER DAY

Carlo Lucarelli was born in 1960 in Modena, Italy. He is the author of eleven noir novels and has been translated into eight languages. *Almost Blue*, the first to be translated into English, was shortlisted for the CWA Gold Dagger for fiction. Lucarelli is the host of a popular television series that examines unsettling and unsolved crimes and the urban centres in which they occur. He also teaches writing in Turin, edits an online magazine, and has written several screenplays.

Oonagh Stransky was born in Paris and went on to live in Beirut and study in Italy and England. She now lives in New York. Her translations include Carlo Lucarelli's *Almost Blue*, Giuseppe Pontiggia's *Born Twice* and Roberto Pazzi's *Conclave*. She won the ALTA Fellow Award in 2000.

ALSO BY CARLO LUCARELLI

Almost Blue

Carlo Lucarelli

DAY AFTER DAY

**TRANSLATED FROM THE ITALIAN BY
Oonagh Stransky**

VINTAGE

Published by Vintage 2005

2 4 6 8 10 9 7 5 3

Copyright © Giulio Einaudi editore 2000, 2004
Translation copyright © Oonagh Stransky 2004

Carlo Lucarelli has asserted his right under the Copyright,
Designs and Patents Act 1988 to be identified as the
author of this work

Published with the financial assistance of the
Italian Ministry of Foreign Affairs

First published in 2000 with the title
Un giorno dopo l'altro by
Giulio Einaudi editore, Torino

First published in Great Britain in 2004 by
The Harvill Press

Vintage
Random House, 20 Vauxhall Bridge Road,
London SW1V 2SA

Random House Australia (Pty) Limited
20 Alfred Street, Milsons Point, Sydney
New South Wales 2061, Australia

Random House New Zealand Limited
18 Poland Road, Glenfield,
Auckland 10, New Zealand

Random House (Pty) Limited
Isle of Houghton, Corner of Boundary Road & Carse O'Gowrie,
Houghton 2198, South Africa

The Random House Group Limited Reg. No. 954009
www.randomhouse.co.uk/vintage

A CIP catalogue record for this book
is available from the British Library

ISBN 0 099 46438 1

Printed and bound in Great Britain by
Cox & Wyman Limited, Reading, Berkshire

For my mother,
who is very different from the one
in this story

DAY AFTER DAY

Pit Bull Terrier (pit bull): A crossbreed of bulldog and terrier conceived in the nineteenth century; used as a fighting dog because of its strong character and athletic build. When dogfights were declared illegal, the breed became more domesticated, developing a sense of loyalty and companionship. Even so, it is said that when a young specimen falls into the hands of an unscrupulous trainer, it instinctively rediscovers the ferocity that makes it "the most dangerous dog in the world".

HE MUST HAVE BEEN THROWN AT LEAST TEN METRES from the car. He could see it behind him on the pavement, wedged between a small lorry with a smashed windscreen and a Volvo, the boot of which had been blown open by the explosion. The car was still burning. He must have been hurled through the glass with the driver's seat and everything, like an aeroplane ejector seat. He must have done a full flip in mid-air because he landed on his back almost in the middle of the junction. He must be dead. The bomb, which blew him out of the car, had torn off both his legs at the knee, and the rest of his body was burnt through to the bone. No, he was still alive. He grabbed Brigadiere Carrone's white bandolier and held on tight, as if he wanted to strangle him. He tried to speak. His lips curled back against his teeth. A red bubble of saliva formed and swelled in the corner of his mouth. He kept his only eye open and stared at the brigadier. He pulled on the bandolier and tried to speak, pushing a scratchy, tense gurgle out of his burnt throat. It felt like his lungs were being ripped out through his mouth.

"It's all right," the brigadier said. "The ambulance is coming . . . just hold on."

The brigadier felt ridiculous saying these words to a man who had been fatally burnt and lost both his legs. At the same time he tried to distance himself. He was used to seeing things like this: he had been in Irpinia after the earthquake, he had spent time in

Kosovo, he was in Capaci when the car carrying Falcone and his bodyguards had been blown up. But this man kept pulling him closer towards his hollow, dry mouth – a mouth that already seemed dead. The brigadier wasn't disgusted. He was scared.

Then the man stopped pulling. His hands slid down the brigadier's cracked leather baldric, leaving a red and black streak on it. He stopped pulling as if he had lost all his strength or as if he wanted to gather it up and use it for something else. Indeed, he leaned his head forward and spat and coughed out a snarl of words.

"Pit bull," he rasped. "Pit bull!"

Brigadiere Carrone thought perhaps there was a dog in the car, on the back seat or shut in the boot. He turned to look at the blackened chassis that still raged with flames. If there had been a dog in the back seat it would be dead by now. The man tugged on the bandolier again, as if he could guess what he was thinking. It wasn't that. There was something else. Brigadiere Carrone looked at the man. However uncomfortable it made him, when a man who has lost both his legs and is dying of third-degree burns tries to speak, someone should listen. So he stopped resisting and let himself be pulled down, his cheek almost knocking into the man's mouth.

He listened to the dry, raspy voice. It was hard to understand. He was so absorbed by it that he didn't even realise that the ambulance crew had arrived. One of them grabbed his shoulder and tried to pull him away from the man.

"Stop!" the brigadier said. "Stop!" he repeated, waving his arm to stop the medic.

"What do you mean, stop?" one of them said.

"Wait a minute," the brigadier said. He slid his hand under the bloody bandolier, into his jacket and pulled out his notebook and pen.

"You two are witnesses," he said to the medics, with a click of his pen. "This is for the record."

SOME SILENCES ARE ACTUALLY FULL OF SOUNDS THAT cancel each other out, that blend together, that become constant, similar, monotonous. Soon you don't even notice those sounds any more. Like a low hum or a soft buzz or the sound of an old car radio that's been out of tune for such a long time it doesn't pick up stations any more. At first it might have just sounded scratchy, but after rasping in your eardrum for long enough, your ear grows desensitised, anaesthetised practically. Or it's like the flat, deaf drone of a car engine that's been travelling at the same speed and in the same gear for a long time. The sound of the engine would break through with an acute sigh, becoming just another one of those bland, dissonant, monotonous notes – virtually nonexistent.

He'd been waiting for such a long time.

The breath of night comes through the air vents, speechless as an open-mouthed sigh. Like the other sounds, it blends and melds with the thick noisy silence that fills the inside of Vittorio's car from windows to roof to floor. The silence presses up against him. It is fluid, like quicksilver, it glides over his clothes, onto his skin, it slips up his nose and into his ears, thin and liquid. It fills up the spaces between the folds of the tissue of his brain.

Thought: I have to have the car checked.

His words echoed in his head, round and clear. They tickled his throat. The back of his tongue. They pushed hard on his larynx when he mouthed them. They rubbed up against his palate noiselessly.

In some kinds of silences it is the unspoken words that resonate the loudest. Not just because of the absence of surrounding sounds. And not just because the silence of solitude had glued his lips, tongue and throat together. It is because of the light. In wintertime there are certain kinds of crisp, chilly mornings when a yell resonates sharper and faster than when it's foggy. Just as there are some days in summertime when the sky is so clear it seems you could see all the way to the other side of the world, and as if sound should be able to travel that far too. And then, when you're at the beach and the sun radiates across the water, you can sometimes hear voices from boats way out at sea; the sounds practically skim along the reverberating light, skipping like stones across the waves. But it's the other way round with unspoken words, the kind that are only thoughts.

For those kinds of words you need darkness.

The darkness of the motorway.

At night the motorway is pitch black. If it weren't for the headlights illuminating the tarmac, the road would be as motionless and dark as a long, sleeping animal, the central reservation like vertebrae jutting out through the animal's skin. If it weren't for the headlights projecting their beams in front of the car, as now, after the rain, and reflecting against the red and yellow crash barriers, if it weren't for the green LED from the radio clawing at the darkness, if it weren't for the dim light from the dashboard revealing his hands on the wheel, if it weren't for the orange indicator blinking in the corner of his left eye each time he turned a corner, if it weren't for these things, everything would be black: him, the car's interior, the road, the air, the sky, even the sea when he drove along by it. The motorway didn't possess its own light. It was like the moon.

It was in this strange, hazy, poorly lit and buzzing penumbra that thoughts – his thoughts – felt strong.

Thought: I need a coffee.

It occurred to him as soon as he saw the road sign that read: AGIP PETROL, 500 MT. He slowed down, only afterwards glancing in his rear-view mirror to check whether anyone was behind him. And someone was. He saw the headlights. They weren't close enough to be dangerous, but close enough to make him belatedly turn on his indicator out of a sense of guilt. He headed into the lane for the services and unfastened his seat belt at the same time; the belt slid up to his shoulder with a snap. The car park was small but empty. He made a wide turn, avoiding the spaces for disabled drivers, and then pulled into a spot and stopped, being careful not to scratch the skirt of the car. He switched off the engine. Only then did he become aware of the man.

He must have been around 30. He was smiling. He walked up to the car with one hand under his jacket, pressed to his chest, and kept the other hand in the air, one finger raised, waving it to get Vittorio's attention and pointing at his jacket, indicating he had something to sell. He continued to smile at Vittorio in a knowing manner. Vittorio shook his head and opened the car door. He had already unhooked the mobile phone from the socket under the dashboard and was ready to show the man that he didn't need another mobile phone, that he already had one, thank you, but by then the man stood with both his hands open in front of him and his expression had changed from a smile to an exaggeratedly sad look, almost offended. He raised one palm in the air, gesturing for Vittorio to wait. He smiled again and raised one finger to indicate that it would only take a second, and then he began the whole pantomime again and would no doubt continue until one of them gave in.

Vittorio sighed. He opened the door and was about to get out of the car to say something to the man, even if he hadn't decided exactly what, when the man grabbed Vittorio's shoulder with his free hand, pushed him back down into the car and pulled a flick knife out of his breast pocket with the other hand. He pressed the cold, jagged blade against Vittorio's cheek, its tip touching his eyebrow. Vittorio held his breath and leaned as far back against the headrest as he could. The man grabbed him by the tie, twisting it around his hand a few times to get a tighter grasp, and leaned halfway into the car.

"Don't move. One word and I'll gouge your eye out."

Vittorio didn't move. He didn't shout. He stayed very still and avoided looking at the man. Under his jacket, clipped to his belt, was a gun, but he hadn't the least thought of reaching for it. Instead, he reached out to the briefcase full of samples on the seat next to him, but the man pressed the blade against his cheek even harder. Vittorio leaned back harder against the headrest. Out of the corner of his eye he saw a car in the rear-view mirror; it was the one that had been behind him when he turned into the service station. It pulled up next to his, the passenger door opened, the motor still running. The man at the wheel looked over at them. The fellow with the knife loosened his grasp on Vittorio's tie and leaned over to get the briefcase of samples. Vittorio thought he ought to show more fear. It didn't seem like he was scared enough.

"Please. Please don't hurt me." He half closed his eyes, not wanting to close them altogether because he didn't trust the man.

"Bastard. Asshole. I hate good-looking pricks like you."

As the man with the knife pulled the briefcase out of the car, the corner slammed into Vittorio's cheekbone, making him cry out. He clenched his teeth to hold still so he wouldn't get cut by the knife. His eyes began to water; he had to shut them.

"Stay right there. Wait until we leave and then you can get out of the car. Careful what you say. I know your route. I can get you whenever I want. We've been watching you for a long time, you bastard."

Vittorio opened his eyes. From behind a veil of shimmery light he saw the man move away. The knife was no longer pressed against his face, but the cold feeling was still there.

"We've been watching you."

He blinked and the feeling was gone. Vittorio was carrying a gun under his jacket, but he wasn't going to use it.

"We've been watching you for a long time, you bastard."

He glanced up through the windscreen at the service station building. From where they were in the car park no-one could see anything. He looked down and noticed the green cover of a guide book in the pocket of his car door, which was still ajar. He grabbed it, stepped out of the car, slipped his hand into his back pocket and pulled out a stiletto knife. He opened it, and just as the man began to turn around, Vittorio flung it into his throat, directly into his jugular vein, holding up the guide book to protect himself from the spray of blood.

As the man collapsed into the getaway car, reaching out to his partner for help, Vittorio was already thinking about what he would tell his mother, how he got the bruise. He knew it was going to be a big one because the whole side of his face ached.

MI SONO INNAMORATO DI TE . . . PERCHÉ NON AVEVO
niente da fare . . .

Is that the way it was? Did I really fall in love with her because I had nothing else to do?

How long can you stay sitting on a swivel chair without moving, with your legs up on the desk, one elbow on the armrest, your head resting in your hand and your eyes shut? How long before millions of invisible ants begin to crawl up your stiff calves? How long before your elbow begins to shoot electric currents down your arm? Before the edge of the table begins to cut into your ankles? How long can you stay like that? Your whole life? Can you stay like that your whole life?

Mi sono innamorato di te . . . perché non potevo più stare solo . . .

My flatmate, aka Morbido, steps into the doorway behind me. He's more fed up than pissed off, "Alex, listen, I've got three things to tell you. First: I can't take this music any more. You know why you're listening to it, don't you? You know, don't you?"

Me: "Because it's beautiful."

Him: "No, because it's sad. And because you're sad. You've been playing this same CD all day long. Well, I'm not sad, I'm feeling pretty good. Look at me. I even have an exam in two days. So turn it down because I have to study. Second: . . ."

Ed ora, che avrei mille cose da fare . . . io sento i miei sogni svanire . . .

". . . we have to pay rent to the signora this week and even if I don't like sticking my nose into other people's business, if your parents are going to send you money only if you take your exams, you should probably start studying. Third: the Problem. He has to go. Right away. Immediately. I mean now. Today. And since we're on the subject, and I know that none of this is my shitty business, in my opinion you're wrong to get all worked up about that girl. Everything has a limit, Alex. She wasn't that special. Life goes on."

He said that last bit out of sympathy, not because he's fed up. He said it with a kind of sadness. But still I don't move. Not until he leaves and shuts the door behind him. I know I'll slide my ankles off the table and hobble over to the stereo, devoured by armies of ants that will make me grab onto the headboard for balance, as if I'm a paraplegic and I've been struck by lightning. But first I'll wait until the song is over. I don't want to give in too easily. And also because what Morbido says isn't true.

Mi sono innamorato di te . . . e adesso non so neppure io cosa fare . . . il giorno mi pento di averti incontrata, la notte ti vengo a cercare.

It's not true that I listen to this stuff only because I'm sad. I really do like Tenco. All right, maybe I especially like his music now because he sings about love stories that have ended but it's not just because of that. The proof is that just when I'm about to turn off the CD I notice a song on the playlist that has nothing to do with love, but it's a good song anyway, so I skip forward to that track and let it play. Then, so as not to upset Morbido, who I know is right, I turn down the music to the lowest level, sit on the floor, and lean my head against the speakers.

The song begins, coming out of the compact silence of the invisible grooves on the CD, with a guitar arpeggio, slowly rising and falling, sweetly hypnotic, barely there. It's as if it wants to end but then gets blurred by a final low note, the same one that begins the next arpeggio, which is identical to the first: sweet and melancholy. Over and over until the song is finished.

It's not true that I live off my parents' money. I work. I have a shitty job, but it's a job all the same. I work for an internet provider, the kind that gives you free access plus a bunch of other things. Its head office is in Bologna. I'm one of the guys who checks the e-mail. I watch out for viruses. I make sure the users don't screw things up, that passwords work, things like that. I'm a kind of virtual night watchman, because I usually work at night, and often from home. Especially recently.

Almost halfway through the third arpeggio Tenco begins to sing. His voice isn't sad, but the words are just about the most devastating words I've ever heard.

Un giorno dopo l'altro . . . il tempo se ne va . . . Le strade sono sempre uguali . . . le stesse case.

Day after day, life drifts away. I earn 900,000 lire a month. It's not a lot, but then, I don't do a whole lot either. I go online for a couple of hours a day, I do what I have to do, and that's that. Things were easier when I used to get money from home, but now that I have to get the 600,000 lire for rent from my wages, it's a little harder. The stereo that I'm listening to, with its half-metre-high Pioneer speakers that I'm leaning against, was the penultimate thing I bought with my wages. "Computer Programming 1" was the last exam I took this year. Since then, the only thing I get from my parents is a hard time.

It's not true that Kristine isn't special . . . and I'm not saying that just because I'm sure I'll never go out with a girl that pretty again. All right, maybe it's just me who sees her that way. Sooner or later the feeling will probably pass and I'll change my mind, but for now it hurts and I don't care about sooner or later.

The only thing Morbido said that was true has to do with the Problem. *That* was the last thing I bought with my wages, even though I couldn't really afford it. But Kristine had seen it at Ivan's house, in the cage with all the other puppies, and Ivan had the stupid idea of telling her that dogs like that are unlucky because if they fall into the wrong hands they become mean and end up getting torn apart in dogfights, even if they really are very sweet by nature. I paid four 100,000 lire notes for him. And he actually is pretty sweet. He spends most of the time sleeping in his box in the bathroom. But he's God-awful ugly, with that flat face of his and small eyes that are set too far apart, almost on opposite sides of his head. I didn't give him to Kristine in time before she left. And now he can't stay here.

E gli occhi intorno cercano quell'avvenire che avevano sognato . . .

There's a part in the song where Tenco's voice breaks. Up until that part he sings in his normal way – his voice seems to come from the deepest part of his throat, it seems to cut through the cigarette smoke he's just inhaled, but it always stays dense and soft just the same. It sounds as if he's perplexed or distracted, or even sad; it sounds as if he must be staring off into the emptiness, like his eyes are barely open, squinting – but then his voice breaks, it gets lower, throatier; it reveals who he really is. He's not thoughtful – he's desperate.

Ma i sogni sono ancora sogni e l'avvenire è ormai quasi passato.

I have to bite my lip. The corners of my mouth droop downwards and I begin to shake. I sniffle because I can't breathe. I breathe irregularly; it hurts. I have to hold my face in my hands and shut my eyes, even if nothing comes out, there's only this great despair. I have to cover my mouth with my hands so that Morbido doesn't hear the low, sad moan that comes out. I squeeze my eyelids tighter shut, but the tears come anyway, and they hurt.

I'm scared.

I'm scared because I feel empty. I feel tired. I don't think I can do anything. I'm only 23 years old, but I feel like I'm two thousand.

I know that all of this has little or nothing to do with Kristine. This is the way things are and that's that. There's no way out.

Day after day.

GRAZIA WOKE UP WITH THE FEELING OF HAVING mumbled something but before she could open her eyes or focus on anything, her words disappeared into a short sigh. The slightest movement of raising her head from the pillow sent a sharp pain through her neck. She closed her eyes and sighed again, this time it was a longer and lazier sigh, more out of protest and desire to go back to sleep. She tried to pull her knees up to her chest and dug one hand under the pillow to reach the other. If she had been in her own bed, at home, in her underwear, she wouldn't have had any problem slipping back into sleep, like dipping a cookie into warm milk. But there, with her jeans tugging at her knees and her spongy sport socks rubbing together, she had to wake up. Suddenly, she was fully conscious of where she was and why she was there. She was lying on her side, in a foetal position, half dressed, on a camp bed in the middle of an unfurnished, damp attic room. She had taken off her jacket and her trainers but had forgotten to take off her watch and while she was sleeping it had pressed into her temple, leaving a mark in the shape of the number seven. It burned. It must have been deep. She felt sure she had said something in her sleep.

Grazia sat up and stayed there for a minute without moving, her arms wrapped around her knees, staring at a point on the wall that began to go out of focus and into a fuzzy grey emptiness that seemed dangerously hypnotic. If she stayed there any longer she would have flipped over onto her side and fallen back to sleep, so she shook her head and rubbed her face and dragged her hands through her hair, arching her back and straightening her T-shirt which had got twisted around her during the night. She got up and walked towards the other room, stopping in the doorway and leaning up against the wall, standing on one foot and scratching the inside of her calf where the elastic of her sock had cut into it.

"Shit, it's about time," sovrintendente Sarrina said, removing his headphones. "I'm allowed to get some sleep, too, aren't I?"

"Uh huh," Grazia mumbled. She went back to the camp bed to get her trainers and her gun, both of which she had left on the floor. When she turned back she had to stop in mid-step, as if she were waltzing, so that Sarrina, who strode with determination into the room, could get past. She sat down on the stool in front of the sound equipment and rested her shoes on the table, thinking that the overall smell in the room wouldn't be much worsened if she left them there. They had been shut in these two rooms of the top floor for three days with no change of clothes and not much more than a sink. Try as they might to tie up the remnants of their sandwiches (two of them would go down to the bar at a time, for supplies) in plastic bags, the smell of rubbish was getting stronger, making itself noticeable under the heavier smell of cigarette butts and stale smoke. Ispettore Matera smoked, as did Sarrina. Once Matera had even produced a cigar. For the time being he was content to hold it and roll it between his fingers, but he wouldn't be able to hold out for too long. He had already begun justifying it, saying that it was a Cuban and that it wouldn't stink the place out like the other ones.

Grazia slipped the headphones on and adjusted them at the base of her neck. The microphone that was hidden in the building across the way whispered its full, buzzing silence: the sound of sleep. She took off the headphones and shrugged.

"Who woke me up?" she asked Matera. His eyes were closed

and his hands crossed over his stomach, his chair tipped all the way back so that he was leaning against the shelf.

"I did," Matera said, without opening his eyes.

"Did I say something?"

"Yes," Sarrina said, from the other room. "You said, 'That's enough, honey, I'm knackered.'"

Matera smiled, keeping his eyes closed. Grazia took one of the small plastic espresso cups that was on the table and threw it at the camp bed, but it was too light and ended up rolling across the floor.

"No, really . . . what did I say?"

"You said, 'Simone, stop, please.' I swear."

Grazia nodded playfully. She looked for another plastic cup on the table, found one and looked inside it. On the bottom was a dark, grainy ring of coffee, a little too dry to be recycled, even in these conditions. But the thermos with the new cups was on the windowsill next to the tripod and video camera, and it seemed so far away. Matera opened his eyes and saw her, her mouth pursed like a child, a subtle frown on her forehead above her dark, heavy eyebrows. He raised his hand to stop her from getting up, but it was too late.

"Don't move," she said. "You might fall over and die. I'll get it myself."

On her way back, absentmindedly twirling a plastic stirrer in her lukewarm coffee, she leaned over the video camera, closed one eye and peered through the viewfinder. The cross hairs of the zoom lens were centred on the front door of the building. The door was closed. It was framed by an ugly cornice of glass cement that reflected the dirty light of the early morning hour. It was 6.30. She was about to take a sip of the coffee when she noticed that the timecode was different from when she had gone to sleep.

"What happened?" she asked Matera.

"Nothing. A boy came home last night and a man went to work

this morning. People live there, you know. Our man's not the only one."

Grazia frowned and pursed her lips again. She pointed to the headphones that were on the table and opened her mouth, but Matera spoke up first, as if he had read her mind.

"No, he didn't go to the third floor. Further up: the fourth or fifth floor. And there were no noises the entire night. We had the headphones on the whole time . . . and besides, it's all taped."

Grazia looked at the surveillance equipment. Its chrome face looked like that of a stereo. There were knobs for regulating the sound levels, a 120-minute tape was slowly turning in the cassette holder and an antenna was linked to the transmitter, which they had planted in the wall of the apartment three days earlier by stopping the lift at the second floor, climbing onto the roof of the cabin through the escape hatch and fixing it in place. The building had thin walls, so that when they removed the buzzing sound of the lift as it passed by, they could hear everything, from the entrance hall almost all the way into the bedrooms.

"Do you think he knows we're here?" Matera asked.

"No," Grazia said. "If we were in Palermo he might, but not here in Bologna. He doesn't have enough of a hold on the territory to keep tabs on the outside elements . . . as long as we stay shut in here, anyway."

"That may be, but it still seems like a bunch of crap to me, Ispettore Negro. If Jimmy Barracu is in there, why don't we just go in and get him?"

Grazia sighed and sat back down. Her coffee was now cold and left a metallic flavour in her mouth, under her tongue. She shivered and shrugged; when she rubbed her feet together she remembered she was still in her socks.

"At first it seemed crazy to me too," she said, pulling her knees up to put her shoes on. "But then Dottore Carlisi explained it to me. He said that when we go in and get Jimmy, the magistrate wants everything: photos of the people who went to see him, even the sounds of him making love to his wife. That way it wouldn't just be chance that we get him and he won't be able to wriggle out of it. Eventually he'll admit it and repent. You know: he'll collaborate, he'll talk."

She turned away from Matera's sceptical expression and put on the headphones over her ears. If it hadn't been for the warmth of the foam rubber and the opaque buzz of the interference, it would be as though she didn't have them on. Mimmo the Fascist, Jimmy Barracu's bodyguard, slept in the room next to the lift. Jimmy and his wife slept down the hall. No-one got up before 10.00, except his wife who woke up at 7.00 to take her medicine, but then went straight back to bed. It was thanks to the wife that they had been able to find Jimmy Barracu. They had tracked the couple halfway across Italy. Grazia had followed the wife from Palermo to Bologna. Now Grazia sat in an attic that they had commandeered from a student, and listened to her sleep.

Grazia brought her hands up to her ears and pressed on the headphones, leaning towards the equipment, as if that would help her to listen in. There was something that wasn't quite right. She said so, but in a whisper, more to herself than to Matera, who had shut his eyes again.

"Something's wrong."

"What did you say?"

"Something's wrong. It's too quiet."

"Everyone's asleep."

"That's just it. No-one's snoring."

Mimmo the Fascist slept directly beneath the microphone that they had planted in the wall. Grazia knew the ugly grunting noises that he made while he slept, sounds that seemed to slide through his mouth and rattle against his teeth, which would then snap shut. The sound wasn't there. There was only a buzzing silence. The grunt wasn't there, nor was the nasal breathing of Jimmy's wife. Even though the room they slept in was all the way down the hall, she made a lot of noise. She was so loud that Grazia wondered how Jimmy managed to sleep next to her.

"No-one came out of the apartment," Matera said. "We would have heard the noise."

A mobile phone was on the table. Grazia pushed it over towards Matera.

"Call Dottore Carlisi. Tell him what's going on."

"Now? Call him to tell him we don't hear anything? He'll be pissed off."

Grazia motioned for him to wait. She looked at her watch. It was 6.59. She shut her eyes and pressed the headphones against her ears, leaning even further forward with her chest, as if she wanted to stick her head into that fuzzy silence. It was almost as if she could smell the silence. It was warm and grey, like the smell of the tape recorder which was turning slowly in front of her, grainy and brightly lit. She waited. She held her breath. And waited.

When the intermittent electronic beep of the alarm went off in the room at the end of the hall – three notes and then a pause – she jumped. The sound was so acute it almost hurt her ears. Then it stopped. Maybe someone had turned it off. Grazia imagined Jimmy's wife's arm reaching out to the alarm clock, fingers fumbling through the air, a sleepy sigh, the thud of her slippers on the floor as she walked to the kitchen, to the drawer where she kept her medicine.

But no. After a pause of 20 seconds the alarm clock started ringing again, this time more insistently. Hysterically.

"Something's wrong," Grazia said again, removing the headphones. "Call the chief. We're going in."

A woman was leaving the building. When she saw them running across the street, armed with their weapons, she pulled back into the doorway and dropped her handbag.

"Don't shut the door!" Grazia yelled out. "Police!"

They entered the entrance hall and ran up the stairs. Matera was the last one to enter; he was older than the other two and slightly overweight. As he ran, Sarrina held his gun in his left hand and grabbed onto the railing with his right. Grazia carried the sub-machine gun, her badge swinging against her bulletproof vest with every step.

There were two doors on the third floor landing. They leaned up against the first one, which someone then opened. "What's going on? Oh God! Mamma!" someone said. By the time Matera turned around, the door was closed.

Jimmy's door was the second one. All three of them stared at it. They glared at it. They held their breath. It was slightly ajar.

"Shit! They can't have left!" Sarrina yelled. "The only way out is the front door . . . they can't have got away!"

Grazia motioned to him with her hand to be quiet. She was the highest ranking officer on that shift and the thought that something might have happened, that Jimmy might have escaped and that it would be her fault for fucking up the entire operation, made her want to cry. Her eyelids stung. She clenched her teeth, tightened the Velcro straps on her bulletproof vest and pushed the door open with the tip of the machine gun.

"Hey, slow down, bambina!" Matera whispered. "What if there's a bomb?"

There was no bomb. In front of them was a long corridor, cloaked in deep grey shadows. Three doors led off of it and there was also a glass door at the very end. The acute intermittent signal from the alarm clock was still ringing. There was a strong, sour smell in the air and it made Grazia bring her hand to her mouth and away from her gun. It was a smell she knew. It was the smell of death.

In the first room on the right, the one that shared the wall with the lift shaft, Mimmo the Fascist was lying on the bed in his underpants and vest. Whoever had cut his throat must have pressed a cushion down on his face at the same time, because it was still there on top of him, lopsided but clean, despite the blood that had drenched everything else: bed, underpants, vest, even the sheets that were tangled around Mimmo's legs, which must have kicked wildly before ceasing to move. In the room at the end of the hall, next to the glass doorway that led to the kitchen, lay Jimmy and his wife. She was on the right side of the bed, her torso and bare shoulders leaning over the edge, one arm drooping down to the ground. He was lying on his back, on the left. One of his hands was resting on her bottom under the covers, the other one gripped at the sheet so tightly that he had pulled it away, revealing a foot. They must have both been shot in the head, and several times, too, because their heads had been blown away.

Grazia leaned against the doorway, lowering the machine gun. The odour, the sight of what they had found and her surprise had taken away her urge to cry, but her legs were trembling. She walked into the room. Without looking at the bed she turned off the alarm clock with the back of her hand. It was then that she saw it, or rather, heard it.

A laptop was softly buzzing on the dresser. The screen had been lowered and when Grazia slowly raised it, the Microsoft logo began to dance from one corner to the next, illuminating the room with a trail of light. Grazia touched the red button of the mouse embedded within the keys and the screensaver disappeared.

In its place appeared the frame of a website that seemed dedicated to dogs. It was so bright that Grazia had to turn her eyes momentarily away.

When she looked again, she found herself face to face with a dog's pointed face. It had brown spots and looked at her with its small, wide-set eyes.

"American pit bull," the writing said under the picture. "The most dangerous dog in the world."

"I DON'T KNOW WHY YOU ALWAYS HAVE TO CUT YOUR hair so short," his mother said, raising her hand towards him.

Instinctively Vittorio pulled back, but then resisted doing so. The muscles in his neck stiffened when she touched the wavy, light blond lock of hair that fell over his forehead.

"You're lucky, you got my hair. You looked good when your hair was longer."

His mother had a rough touch. Her hands were small, thin and well manicured, but they felt heavier than they looked. More than touching, she pushed at him, she pressed, as if needing to make sure he was all there, nearby, within reach. Vittorio's neck muscles stayed stiff until he felt his mother's cold fingertips pull away from his scalp like a receding wave, and then he shrugged with indifference.

I like my hair like this.

But his mother was already thinking about the steak that was gently frying on the stove, about the fork that she would need to stick into it to flip it over, about the salt that needed to be added, about the drops of blood that were evaporating on the hot metal. For some reason she wanted to believe that Vittorio liked his meat well done. He had never been able to convince her otherwise. Nor had he been able to convince her to stay on the sofa in the living room watching television when he came home at 10.00 or 11.00. It was useless for him to try and protest that at 30 years of age he knew how to cook a steak for himself. She would get up in the middle of the film and come into the kitchen to cook him dinner. And, if he tried to insist, she would reply that they saw so little of each other, that he was never home, that it would be good for them to talk. But she was the one who did all the talking. Vittorio could barely bring himself to answer.

"Here you go – well done, just the way you like it. Watch out now, or I might burn you. Salad or tomatoes? A few vegetables would be good for you. Who knows what you eat when you're on the road. Are you sure you're not working too hard? You look tired. Don't make me worry, all right? So, what'll it be: salad or tomatoes?"

"Tomatoes."

He was already thinking about something else. He was thinking about a nose, about an old man's nose that he had seen earlier in the day. He even managed to visualise it as he was cutting his dry, overcooked meat, staring at a point on the chequered tablecloth. It would be a broken nose, with a lowered septum, flattened in the middle and bent a little to the left. It would be the nose of a man who had been through a lot, a man who had seen brutal, ugly, rough things.

His mother pulled out a chair and sat down, resting her arms on the table.

"Can you hear the Festa dell'Unità? Everyone on our street complained that it was too loud. Now it's so quiet you can barely hear it. Right? You can barely hear it."

"Yes. You can barely hear it."

"Annalisa said that she called you, but that your mobile was turned off. I don't think you're taking very good care of her. You're not leading her on, are you? When will you see her next? Will you see her tomorrow night?"

"Yes, I'll see her tomorrow night."

"Are you going to be home all week? If you are, we could go and see Papa. How long is it since you've seen Papa – a month?"

"Yes, I'll be home this week."

"Should we go see him tomorrow morning? Is tomorrow morning all right?"

"Yes."

"Have you finished here? Can I take your plate?"

"Yes.

"Have some tomatoes; they're good for you."

"All right."

"I'm going back to watch the end of the film. Leave everything here and I'll take care of it in the morning."

"All right."

Vittorio waited for his mother to leave the kitchen and then he served himself three slices of tomato, ate one, drove the fork into another and then got up from the table.

"Are you going to your room? Don't stay up too late; you're tired."

Vittorio didn't answer. He went down the dark corridor and climbed the stairs to the second floor. The bluish flickering light from the television lit his way. He knew exactly where to step; he didn't even touch the end of the stair with his foot. The seventh step creaked, as always. The corridor upstairs was dark. The light from the television didn't reach up there, but Vittorio knew the way to his bedroom. *La cameretta*, as his mother called it.

He turned on the desk lamp only after he had shut the door behind him. First he stood in the middle of the room until his eyes got used to the shadows, until he could make out the crucifix hanging above the bed, the little ceramic guardian angel, the two posters: one of New York by night and the other of windsurfers. His mother was right, the noise and the music from the Festa dell'Unità were barely audible, even though the celebrations were taking place just a street away, on the football field at the edge of the neighbourhood where their house, and the row of single family villas just like theirs, was situated. Vittorio opened one of the two desk drawers and took out a plastic model aeroplane, a Messerschmitt 262 from WWII, an Airfix model on a scale of 1:150. He rested it on the desk, with the fuselage open. The nacelle still needed to be mounted. He tipped it forward slightly so that the pilot could be inserted with a pair of long-nosed tweezers, which he promptly placed next to the model together with the superglue, the pliers and the file, for scraping away surplus bits of glue. Then he pushed everything into a corner of his desk. He took a key from his pocket and unlocked the other drawer. He opened it and looked at the nose.

It wasn't finished yet. It wasn't the way he needed it to be. He took the latex form out of its box, peeled it off a plaster of Paris mould of his nose and placed it over his real nose, smoothing down the edges onto his cheekbones and holding it still between his eyes so that it wouldn't fall. It was a perfect fit. Even the small straws that he had planted in the nostrils, where the nasal passages would be, fit directly into his own. It was as if that large whitish protuberance had grown on his face all by itself. But no, it still wasn't quite right. Not yet.

He put the latex sheath back around the plaster mould. Holding it tightly in one hand, he pulled off a pinch of plasticine from the block that he kept in the box, rubbed it between his fingers until it was soft and then stuck it onto the middle of the septum, moulding it to shape. With his nail he scratched off another piece of plasticine and attached it to the left of the septum, just where the bump ended.

He picked up the nose, pinching the nasal passage between his thumb and index finger, his elbow resting on the desk. He closed one eye and observed it carefully under the light. Now it was perfect. The newly added parts fitted exactly. Only the contrast in colour between the dark grey plasticine and the opaque white of the latex revealed that there was anything artificial about the nose.

Now all he would have to do is to cover it with plaster to get a uniform mould, then pour latex into it through the canals until it was the right thickness. He wanted an old man's nose, a nose that was swollen and deformed with age, broken down by life.

On the staircase outside his room, he heard the seventh step creak loudly, as always. Vittorio laid the nose inside the wooden box and drew the model aeroplane towards him. It had been a long time since his mother came into the *cameretta* without knocking, but he was convinced that it was good for him to put his defence routine into practice each time there was the risk; it helped him stay alert.

His mother, from the hallway: "I'm going to bed. Don't stay up too late. You're tired."

He waited for the sound of her bedroom door closing. Then he peeled back the strip of latex from the mould, spread a thin layer of rubber cement on the edge, just a little bit, just enough for it to stick by itself, and he put it on. Something was still missing.

With the nose still on his face he took a long metal hook from his wardrobe, opened the trapdoor that led to the attic and pulled down the retractable ladder. He never liked going up into the attic, maybe it was because the ceilings were too low, or because the windows started down at the floor. He went there only to do the most dangerous and riskiest jobs, such as modifying the silencer on his Brügger+Thomet with a layer of soft felt discs, which he had taken from the suction filter of an outboard motor. He kept the gun on a shelf in the attic, wrapped in a rag, together with the Sig Sauer .9 calibre, on which he was modifying the barrel. But now he opened the window and sat on the ledge, looking out over the Festa dell'Unità with his Swarovski binoculars, his breathing whistling quietly through the plastic straws.

From that side of the house the music was louder. It was still far away, and it still got distorted as it reverberated off the houses –

the high sounds filtered out over the distance, but the lower, aggressive, throbbing sounds made it across. Subsonica was performing: "All my mistakes".

He looked for an old man in the crowd. Just the right kind of old man. He tilted the binoculars into position and adjusted the knobbled dial until he got a clear, round field of vision. He left the main area, where the concert was going on, because it was full of young people. He skimmed to the beer stand and the food court, where meals were still being served. The music was completely detached from what he could see through the binoculars: it sounded even more abstract, out of sync. It was like watching a television on which the volume had been turned down while listening to the radio.

you know how to protect and how to hurt me
kill me and then start in again
catch me alive
you are all of my mistakes

He looked around the tables, behind the serving area and near the grills, but no-one particularly caught his eye. And then someone did. A man was getting up from the table, near the serving area. He was holding a tray piled high with plastic plates in one hand and removing his apron with the other. A wooden toothpick hung from the corner of his mouth. Vittorio noticed this particular detail, and stored it away in his memory for another time. Right now it was of no use to him. He was probably a volunteer at the food court and had just finished eating his meal after working a shift at the tables. That wasn't important to Vittorio either, though he directed his binoculars at the leftovers on the plate, more out of curiosity and habit than necessity. Tortellini with meat sauce, polenta with sausage, a half carafe of red wine and a *zuppa inglese*. No water or coffee. He waited for the man to move, because that was what interested him most. His speed, his rhythm – the things he had learned about in his most recent acting class. Then he saw it. The man took tight, quick steps that seemed to finish too abruptly, as if he held something back. He pushed at the air with the elbow of his free arm when he walked. Vittorio observed the way the old man held his tray: evenly, steadily, but with thick, heavy fingers, he balanced the tray in the air more than held it. He watched the way he turned his head towards the counter, with a slow half turn, like the turret of a tank. He *was* like an old tank, an old factory worker, an old artisan or an old farmer who still had a lot of energy, but whose body responded jerkily and then gave out altogether.

You drown so you can breathe
learning how to bleed
each day that slips away
real time: that's you

Thought: A man like that, one who makes those kinds of movements and who has a nose like the one I now have. A man like that would probably wheeze a little. I'd have to open the holes in the latex, but not a lot, just at the top, so that I wouldn't be able to breathe freely.

With that detail in mind, he rested his head back against the window sill and smiled in satisfaction.

You, my pride, you can wait
and even when there's more pain
I can't complain
I can't give up
all my mistakes.

THEY NEEDED ANOTHER CHAIR. SARRINA GOT UP TO fetch one, but the door to the next office was blocked by the cart for the audiovisual equipment. He started to head off somewhere else, but Dottore Carlisi yelled out, "Forget it! We're not at the movies!" and Matera said that he would stand because his back hurt anyway. He leaned against the wall, his hands flat behind his bottom. At that point, Sarrina was already halfway across the room so he stayed where he was, near the door. Grazia sat on a metal stool, on top of a heap of legal papers, in the corner furthest from the commissioner. From where she was sitting she couldn't see the monitor clearly – it was washed out by the light that poured in through the window, and which they had tried to screen by moving the cart. With everything that had gone on after they entered the apartment she hadn't had time to shower and she was a little embarrassed to be so close to her commanding officer. And after the failure of the operation, she just wanted to be forgotten.

"We'll talk about the mess you've made, and its consequences, later," the commissioner began. "Now everyone be quiet and listen to this. It's very strange. Sasa', come over here and turn this thing on."

Ispettore Di Cara had arrived from Palermo earlier that afternoon. He had come directly from the airport to the Bologna Mobile Unit to examine the cassettes and videotapes that Grazia and her team had recorded while they occupied the small attic room across the street from Jimmy's apartment. He had stayed there, in the office where they were all now gathered, for more than four hours. When he bent down in front of the equipment on the cart, Grazia, Matera and Sarrina all leaned towards the television before realising that the inspector had turned on only the audio function.

"We can determine the precise moment at which the murders took place. Mimmo the Fascist: 0347," he said, raising a finger towards one of the speakers. A repressed hiss, a flat gurgle, a rapid whoosh, and then silence.

"The other two: 0351 and 21 seconds."

Two hiccups, almost at the same time. Only one whoosh.

"Careful, here comes another." One more hiccup, but thinner, opaque, slow.

"I'd like to know which of you was on duty at that time," the commissioner said.

"I was," Sarrina replied. "But I didn't . . ."

"I was too," Matera said, "I couldn't sleep at all. I heard those noises, the last ones, but they seemed like a sigh, like someone turning in their sleep."

"Actually they were three glass bullets encased in plastic, .22 calibre at a high speed, judging from the effect. Silenced," Di Cara said. "And a convulsion. But don't take it badly. You can hear them now because they've been amplified and cleaned with the equaliser. I wouldn't have noticed them either, without headphones."

"Thank you, Di Cara," the commissioner said. "But don't be too soft on them. The man that they were supposed to be watching got killed. Three murders during someone's watch. Sounds like a real cock-up to me. But we'll talk more about that later."

Grazia sat on the stool, leaning forwards, her elbows on her knees. She bit the inside of her mouth and pressed her cheek with her finger. She could well imagine the scene. Whoever had killed Jimmy and his wife and bodyguard must have used night vision goggles to move through the apartment silently, without bumping into anything: slipping through a labyrinth of green lines and bright outlined shapes to get close enough to Mimmo to slit his throat. The person who had done the shooting, a second man perhaps, must have had a laser guide installed under the barrel of the gun to fire with such precision. A red light that shines out of the shapeless mass of the silencer, a Brügger+Thomet or a Mark Withe Millennium, maybe wrapped in a damp rag. A red spot of light that dances on the green head, and that is suddenly still. One bullet for each of them – and then the final shot for Jimmy. He must have also applied a screen to the bolt of the gun to catch the falling shells, because they hadn't found any in the apartment. She could visualise it all except one thing.

"How did they get in? There's only one entrance and we would have heard the noises from the break-in. Or at least, we should have heard them."

"Three twenty one," Di Cara said, bending down in front of the recording equipment and lightly touching the rewind button, then shaking his head. "Never mind, I'll tell you what happened. At 0321 you hear something metallic. Very, very faint. I only realised it after looking at the fluctuations on the soundtrack. Nineteen minutes later, another sound: the chain, a tiny bit louder, but still soft. It took him 19 minutes to pick the lock, going a millimetre at a time. Then he picked up the chain with a pair of curved tweezers and took another seven minutes to loosen it."

"Christ," Matera murmured. "That's patience."

The commissioner looked at Ispettore Di Cara, who smiled.

"But that's not all," Di Cara said. "Can you guess why he did it so slowly? Yes, to be quiet, because he didn't want to wake up the people inside. But why specifically so slowly?"

"Because he knows we're listening to him," Grazia said. "He knows we're listening and that we have better ears than Jimmy and his people. That's why he stands still for 20 minutes to pick the lock."

"Bravo," Di Cara said.

"Bravo bullshit," the commissioner said. "Di Cara, that girl is an expert at catching criminals. Before coming to the Mobile Unit she was with me in Rome; I swear she's a bloodhound. When we were after someone she would stare at his picture endlessly. She never slept, she studied him, she knew everything he did, everything he said, what he was like when he was a kid, what he dreamed about. Shit, it was like the killer was her boyfriend. Only instead of marrying him she threw him in jail. I gave her this job for a reason – and then she pulls this crap on me. Bravo, Grazia, well done!"

Grazia didn't say anything. She looked at the ground, her lips tightly shut, her chin trembling with anger.

Matera pulled his hands out from behind his back and took a cigar out of his shirt pocket. He wasn't going to smoke it. As soon as they walked into the commissioner's office he said that the room was too small, he didn't want to be the only one to smoke, but he wanted to hold it. He was about to repeat himself, but he was distracted by a thought, a bothersome thought, a thought that made him uneasy.

"Now, hold on," he said. "If you think these people knew about us, fine . . . but if you think they noticed us while we were there, well, I have some problems with that. I watched what was going on and I never saw anyone in ambush. When we went down to eat or when we went out, I never saw anyone more than once and I never saw anyone act suspiciously."

"You wouldn't have noticed," the commissioner said. Matera stepped away from the wall and stood up straight, having taken offence. His nose and the skin under his eyes suddenly became red, like a mask. He squeezed the cigar tightly between his fingers, making it crackle.

"I'm sorry, Commissario, but I refuse to let you . . ."

"Don't get angry with me, Matera," the commissioner interrupted. "I'm not just saying things. Watch this and you'll see what I mean."

Ispettore Di Cara went back to the audiovisual cart, squatted down on his haunches and turned on the video recorder. Grazia got up from the stool where she was sitting and went to the desk so that she could see the screen without the glare. She rested her hand on top of the backrest of the commissioner's chair, close to his shoulders, and leaned forwards. She no longer cared that she hadn't taken a shower in three days.

The tape was in position. An image of the front door of the building where Jimmy had been hiding out appeared on the screen. The door was closed. The white numbers on the timer in the right-hand corner of the screen changed rapidly. The seconds sped on to 0310.

"The building is a typical 1970s unit . . ." Di Cara started to say.

"We know all about it," Sarrina interrupted. "We spent three days staring at it. Twin blocks, each with their own entrance hall and stairwell. No other entrances. Six floors per block, two apartments per floor. Jimmy rented both the apartments on his floor."

Di Cara sighed. He leaned forwards and stopped the tape. The image was the same, the front door, framed by concrete and glass tiles, a bit of road in front of the building, illuminated by a pale cone of light, surrounded by static shadows.

"Easy now," Di Cara said, still on his knees, his finger on the button of the recorder. "I'm not nit picking. I just wanted to tell you that at least 50 people live in each of those blocks, so that even if the Mobile Unit screened all the neighbours to see if there is someone on your tape that doesn't live in the building, you should still take it with a pinch of salt."

He pressed a button and took a quick breath, tired from squatting all that time. He returned to his chair and leaned against the backrest. The tape began to turn.

"Grazia, in your opinion, how many people did it?" the commissioner asked.

There was something on the video, something arriving in the corner of the frame. Grazia didn't take her eyes off the screen. She stopped biting the inside of her cheek.

"At least two," she said. "No-one left to stand watch outside, otherwise Sarrina would have seen them." But she didn't sound very sure of herself.

"In fact, we have two suspects," Di Cara said. "Here's the first one."

It was a boy on a bike. A change in the light of the shadows on the street signalled his arrival. He was somewhere between 20 and 25. A student, probably. Tall, thin, with long, wavy hair which was tied in a loose knot at the base of his neck. He wore a faded brown ribbed jumper and reddish trousers. Trainers. A black rucksack hung loosely on his back. He had a thin, slightly ginger, curly beard. His hair was the same colour. He leaned his bike against the wall of the building, on the road, at the edge of the frame, and wrapped a chain around the handlebar and through the wheel, hooking it onto something that was out of the field of vision. He pulled out some keys and entered the building.

"That's the first one," Di Cara said, stopping the tape and fast forwarding it. "Ten minutes later the noises on the door began. But later on, another man comes out."

"I remember him," Matera said.

"I remember him, too," said Sarrina. "There was nothing strange about him."

"Apart from the fact that he came out 20 minutes after the last

32

shot was fired. But that's not the point. Look at him," Di Cara said.

The timer now showed 0410. A man of about 50 came out of the front door. He was short and heavy set; he had greyish hair that was slicked back over his round head. He was balding. He wore a blue tracksuit under a grey puffer jacket that had faded yellow and red stripes on the sleeves. He had a cigarette in his mouth and held an old, faded sports bag in his hand. He stopped for a moment on the threshold to take a drag on his cigarette, his fingers gripping the filter tightly, his eyes half shut, a corner of his mouth open in an unpleasant grin. Then he flicked the cigarette butt away with his middle finger. Get the butt. Run a DNA test on the saliva.

"Hold on," Matera said. "The boy that tied up the bike when he went in . . . that doesn't seem like something a person would do before he kills three people."

The commisioner smiled. He leaned back in the chair and linked his hands behind his neck. Grazia suddenly found him between her arms and she jumped back, but no-one noticed.

"Tell them Sasa'," the commissioner said, with a sigh. "Tell them and let's bring this meeting to an end."

"I took a little time to play with the program that you have at headquarters for making facial comparisons."

Grazia nodded, as if he was talking directly to her, even though Di Cara kept his gaze on the commissioner. She knew the program he was talking about. It picked up certain traits in people's faces. It digitalised a photograph or a photogram, it calculated the distance between people's eyes, the angle of the nose, the length of the hair, the shape of the ears, and it reduced all the information to numerical formulae so that it could be compared with other faces that had undergone similar analyses. Eighty per cent of criminals were identified in this way.

"I compared the data with people who already have a record," Di Cara went on to say. "Nothing. Neither of these two men have any penal precedents. No murder, theft, nothing. Clean. Unknown. But that's not what's strange. It was Dottore Bozzi's idea. We ran the program on the images of the man and the boy, and you know what? They're the same person."

The commissioner pulled two photographs out of a folder on his desk: the boy on the bike and the man in the track suit. The enlargements were black-and-white, grainy and opaque, with dotted lines and red pen marks on the immobile faces.

"Holy fuck . . ." murmured Sarrina. "How can that be?"

Grazia leaned down and looked at the photographs. They looked like two entirely different people. They were two different people. Totally different.

"Matera," the commissioner said, without looking over at him. "I'm sorry, but you'll have to cancel your holiday plans. You'll have to wait to see that Cuban woman of yours. We fucked up and now we have to fix it. We have a professional killer on our hands, someone who is capable of changing his identity at will, someone who works on his own, who never makes mistakes, even if we have the victims under surveillance. Negro." He looked at Grazia, who looked back at him, attentively. "This is your job. Bring me that man."

Grazia nodded, without saying a word. She followed Matera and Sarrina out of the door, stepping over a chair that had been knocked down. Di Cara spoke in a whisper, but she heard it clearly enough.

"Commissioner, are you sure that that girl has the balls for something like this?"

"IT'S NOT A PIT BULL."

"But it looks like one.'

"It's not a pit bull. It's a Staffordshire bull terrier. It looks like a pit bull, but it's not. He's very gentle. They're the gentlest dogs in the world."

"That may be, but it looks like a pit bull to me. Keep it tied up, would you, please?"

It's always the same thing. When I take him out for a walk, people in the street drag their children out of the way and pick up their dogs. They glare at me as if to say "Here comes that guy with the mean dog," but they never say anything. If they did, if they insulted me, for example, I would explain to them that this dog is nothing more than a sausage with legs, that all his mouth ever does is devour two cans of disgusting food each day, whatever is on special offer at a thousand lire per can. And what looks like a sneer on his face is really nothing more than a dumb smile, the kind that belongs to animals who sleep 23 hours a day and eat, piss and shit during the remaining hour. But no-one ever dares say anything. They look at me like I'm a lunatic. I refuse to go around with a sign on my neck that says, "He's not a fucking pit bull!"

Luckily some people understand. Morbido, for example. Even though he doesn't want him in the house, he doesn't have any other problems with him. Maybe because he doesn't really know what a pit bull is. Here at Freeskynet, on the other hand, they just don't get it. The first night I brought him here, it was a mess. My boss told me never to do it again, and Luisa doesn't believe that he's not a pit bull, for chrissakes.

I'll hurt you more than a gun shot
and that's barely what you deserve.

"Keep him a little closer to you, would you? I'm practically falling off the chair as it is. Look, Alex, I can't even reach the keyboard."

Luisa is downloading the Subsonica concert recording from the Festa dell'Unità. Not live; the concert was yesterday. Actually, more than downloading it, she's watching it, because she likes Subsonica. I like Subsonica too, but I'd rather be listening to Tenco right now.

How would things be after a gunshot
You'd be a little lost

"Either put him on a shorter lead or move to another terminal! Christ! He's almost next to my leg!"

"Let's switch: I'll come do the music."

"No way, you're in charge of the chat rooms, sweetie."

She's right. Checking the chat rooms might not be the most boring job at the provider, but it is definitely the most tiring. Freeskynet Bologna has three rooms on the second floor of an old palazzo in the city centre. The first room is for the secretary and the person in charge of customer service, registration, marketing and so on. The second room, which is right next door, is the director's. It's a small room, but he likes it that way. The third room is for us: we're the heart of the operation. In here are the desks and terminals, the shelves with modems, this is where the slaves create the web pages, upload and download files, where we make sure everything works properly. Above all, the chat rooms and the e-mail. There are three of us: me, Mauri and Luisa. Or rather, in order of importance: Mauri, Luisa, me.

This whole time
I vomited bitterness
I sewed together the parts
I began to hope again

Right now I wish I didn't have to do a damn thing. I'd like to
fold my arms over the keyboard and rest my head on them, with
my nose on the z key and sleep forever, an infinite number of
*zzzzzzz*s appearing on the screen. I'd like to spend the rest of my
life sleeping. Day after day. Really. The last thing I want to do
right now is take care of the chat rooms and make sure
everything works, that the users follow the rules, that no-one
creates a room to talk about things that are illegal. And, above
all, make sure there are no paedophiles. Not now, anyway. Not
with all those stories in the newspapers. Once the bad guys were
the skinheads, then the Satanists, now it's the paedophiles. The
director told us to keep an eye out for them. He even made us
put a warning on the home page, next to the logo for the chat
rooms: "Warning: Net Patrol! Anti-paedophile Surveillance!"
That's supposed to be me. Night watchman, electronic postman
and cyber cop, fighting paedophilia. As if it were actually
possible to spot a paedophile, here, between these lines in
Helvetica 14 point, that come shooting out after one another
across the screen:

Cl@udia: ciao! how old are you?

M@xbonissimo: what do you do?

Robert@: who r u?

auror@: where r u writing from?

Debby: :-)

Roby: ;-)

Kitty: :-(

Patty: :-(((

If you click on their names sometimes you can read a profile
about them, when they've chosen to create one. But right now I

don't care about anybody else's story. I'm too wrapped up in my own.

Sadguy87: (4 Mara, i luv u)

Ramones88: (pissedoff)

Smokey86: (bumalek bumalek shivaaaa!)

"Hey Luisa, do you usually leave your boyfriends or do they leave you?"

"I leave them."

"And do you ever regret it afterwards? I mean, do you change your mind?"

"Never."

"Thanks, Luisa."

She realises she was a bit harsh, because she turns and looks at me. I look at her too. She's not bad, Luisa. Twenty-five, petite, well built. Cute. Her hair is light, wavy, shoulder length. She's wearing one of those ethnic types of necklace, made of bones and other tubes, sort of American Indian. She's still got a tan as if she just came back from holiday. She's got on a couple of bracelets, too, the African kind, and a few rings made of plaited silver. Her fingernails are short. She's smoking. Extra thin Merits. She's wearing khaki army trousers, with lots of pockets, that are loose around the ankles, and a brick-red vest top. Our boss saves money on air conditioning. She's wearing sandals that are scrunched down at the back and her toenails are painted dark blue. She has a fine silver chain around her ankle. I don't think I've ever looked at her so closely before.

"Look, she's not the only woman in the world," she says. "And you're not the only unlucky bastard in the world. Sooner or later you'll find someone else."

"You think so?"

"Yes."

"You want to go out with me tomorrow?"

"No."

"Thanks, Luisa."

This time she doesn't look at me. She shrugs and goes back to watching the Subsonica concert in the small square in the centre of her screen, full colour, but grainy, where the singer and musicians move around smoothly and frantically, slightly out of sync with the music.

You had everything
even my best dream . . .
you took everything I had
with no holding back, no honour

I rock back in the armchair, slowly, so I don't tip over and I link my hands behind my neck. I look up and stare at a patch of mildew lurking in a corner of the ceiling. Like many of the *palazzi* in the centre of Bologna, this one has frescoed ceilings, or rather, it would have them, if only someone would remember that they exist.

"Actually," I say, "She was the most beautiful girl in the world."

"Well, how about that," says Luisa, almost to herself.

"No, she was really beautiful. Blonde, Danish, blue eyed. But not your usual Nordic blonde, no, she had an unusual face. Her nose was slightly crooked . . . sort of a blend between Cameron Diaz and Ellen Barkin. She broke her nose when she was little."

I touch my own nose, it's straight and narrow. I wish I could feel the same bump in my nose that she had. I miss her nose.

"One of her eyes was a shade lighter than the other, one was cornflour blue and the other was deep azure. And her ears, too. When she pulled her hair up you could see that one stuck out a little more than the other. It was because she always slept that way when she was little, in her cot. And one of her collarbones, here . . ." and I touch myself on my neck, but it's not the same thing, "one stuck out a bit more."

"In other words she was all crooked."

"Fuck you, no. She was . . . harmonious. Unusual."

"Original, you mean."

"No, not original, Luisa, beautiful. Kristine was beautiful, not original."

I say it too loud, with too much emphasis. Dog wakes up under my desk and raises his head. He opens his jaws and part of his tongue slips out: pink, thin and wet. He looks around with his small, widely spaced eyes, one on each side of his pointed head, with that expression he has that resembles a child with Down's Syndrome. Luisa pushes her chair back from the desk and pulls her legs up next to her, pointing her toes. She does it so quickly that one of her sandals slides off and falls to the floor. Dog would like to get it and pulls on his lead, but quietly, without exerting himself.

"Keep that beast away!" Luisa says.

"He won't hurt you . . ."

"Call him back! He has a name doesn't he? Didn't she give him one before she left you?"

To tell the truth, no, she didn't. And I didn't even think about it. Morbido calls him the Problem. I call him Dog. But in that particular moment, I couldn't care less about his name.

"She didn't leave me," I say. "I mean, not really. She was here with a study abroad programme, for a year. Then the year ended and she went back to Copenhagen. End of story."

Dog is still a little undecided about whether to continue to try and get Luisa's sandal or just give up. He must decide it isn't worth it, because he lowers himself back down onto the floor, right where he is, and falls asleep. She glares at me, takes one more puff of her cigarette, puts it out, and then points to my screen.

"Looks like you've crashed," she says meanly.

She's right. The chat rooms have become disconnected; they don't highlight any more when I click on them with the mouse. Even some of the windows don't highlight when I click on them. They're inert. I put my hands on the keyboard and activate the message that asks the users to disconnect and reconnect and then I do everything that has to be done to get things back the way they should be.

Buffy: What a bomb!

Debby: Ouch!

Poppy: Are u there?

The chat area at Freeskynet has about 50 rooms in it. The list of rooms can be found in a rectangle at the top of the screen and when you scroll down the list it shows you the nicknames of the people that are in it. Some of the rooms – luckily only a few of them – are moderated, which means that someone watches over them: namely me. I animate the conversation when it starts to lag, I have to be careful that they don't use too many bad words, I have to throw out the usual bastard who goes into the room with things like: "Looking for a slut to screw – anyone interested?" Each room has its own odd, captivating, obscene name: kids.chat, IceMoon, The Kingdom of Avalon, Filippos friends.chat, but most of them are sexual in nature: sex.chat, oralsex.chat, analsex.chat, shitinmymouth.chat, even one called jerkoffwithmewhileitalkaboutmygirlfriend.chat. There's only one user in that room, jerk27, who's waiting in the left-hand corner. There are four s&m rooms and they're always full. There are 15 gay and lesbian rooms, 8:7 in favour of the girls. Some people use the chat rooms in place of the telephone, like worker31, who always ends with, "got 2 go girls, boss is back". Then there are those who are looking for something specific, people who ask for photos, webcam images, e-mail addresses and mobile phone numbers. Immediately. Serious enquiries only. Then there are those who play around, who invent a name and act the part, such as Casanova32cm, Dirtygirl, YoungReinhardtSS, MisterMaster and his humble slave (who writes everything in lower case because slaves aren't allowed to use capital letters in their nickname). In these chat rooms, hardly anyone speaks in public, where their words would fall into a common area when they hit ENTER, one after another, full of mistakes because of their hurry to type. No, these kinds of conversations almost always take place in private: all they have to do is double click on the name in the corner square and they can speak directly with the person they want in their own room, alone and invisible to others.

Or at least that's what they think.

But it's not true.

I can read them.

My nickname has a series of commands attached to it that give me the power to do almost anything I want. Like entering into the private rooms, without being seen. That way I can watch.

Cornelius: Can you feel my hands on you? Can you feel my hands around your neck? Can you feel them covering up your mouth?

Lara: yes, I feel them.

Cornelius: Can you feel my shaft inside you? I'm pushing your back up against the wall, Lara. I'm pushing so hard, Lara . . .

Lara: I can feel it Cornelius . . . push harder, let me wrap my legs around your thighs . . . push harder, now . . .

The cybersex is always pretty soft. I always wonder what the people are doing at that particular moment. Are they touching themselves? Are they really getting excited? Or are they in their offices, sitting perfectly composed, pretending to work?

Sade: Come on, slave: I'm going to whip you now. Thwhack thwhack thwhack!

Justine: let me lick you, master. let me lick you!

Masoch: Yes, hurt me, ahhh! Ahhh! Here I cuuumme!

Venus in Fur: You know that recipe you gave me the other day? Do I use all the vegetables, even carrots?

It's not really in my nature to be a voyeur. At the beginning it was fun to look into the rooms like some kind of Big Brother and learn about other people's shit and how strange the world really is, but then it gets boring. I have my own problems to deal with. Now I'm jumping from one chat room to another, like when I have to take an exam and I can't study for it because the mere thought of it makes me feel extremely tired, so instead I waste time by looking out the window or turning on the TV or surfing the net. Only for 15 minutes, I promise.

Luisa must have asked me if I would give her a hand or something like that because I look over at her screen and see that the Subsonica concert has frozen into a series of superimposed images. I tell her I can't, not because I want to be a jerk but because of that painfully sad feeling I get when I know there's something that has to be done, and especially now, when I don't want to be doing anything except listening to Tenco and thinking about Kristine. So, in order to give myself a reality check I leave the erotic rooms and go and look in the more normal ones, which are, in fact, probably stranger. I move the arrow of the cursor into the lower right-hand corner and refresh the list of rooms, which is constantly changing because people can open their own and close them when they like. I notice there's a new one that makes me sit up in my chair and peer into the screen.

It's called pitbull.chat.

In the right-hand rectangle there are two nicknames, one above the other: PitBull and OldMan.

I glance at Dog, who's asleep on the floor. He looks dead. I go into the room in secret, so my name doesn't show up.

Nothing. Empty screen. Nothing is being written. PitBull and OldMan are writing to each other in private.

Luisa says something again, but I shake my head, whatever it is. I have my fingers on the keyboard and my mouse ready. I look for them, find them and enter.

OldMan: Is my pit bull ready?
PitBull: Almost.

OldMan: They called. They want to hurry. They want it right away.

I look at Dog. I look at Luisa's sandal which has fallen only a centimetre away from his nose. As soon as he wakes up he'll probably start chewing on it. And she will probably start screaming.

PitBull: They'll get it when it's ready.

OldMan: Soon.

OldMan: There's no more time.

I'd like to enter the chat room and tell him that I have a dog like that. A dog that's pure and beautiful; I'd even give it to them for free. Right away. Wherever they are, in Pordenone, Palermo, wherever. I'd even bring it to them. Immediately, with Morbido's car. He could drive me. Should I do it? If I enter the room all hell will break loose, I'd lose my job and I'd probably even break the law.

OldMan: It's a fierce job. We need the genuine article.

OldMan: We need a pit bull.

Shit.

OldMan: It won't be easy.

OldMan: You know that, right?

Pit Bull: I know.

There's something strange about this conversation. Something worrisome. I look at the screen and suddenly shiver. I don't know why. I have to remember to save it before I close my contact with the chat room.

OldMan: You know what I want.

OldMan: The best . . .

OldMan: The very best . . .

PitBull: I know

[Sunday, September 17, 02:09:30 Pdt 2000] PitBull left private chat.

The chat closes precisely at the moment Luisa manages to

unblock the Subsonica concert. The music explodes into the room. She must have made a mistake when she was working on the audio files and raised the volume to the loudest level. From her terminal's speakers the nasally voice of the singer, enlarged and distorted by volume, assaults me. It's sharp and jarring: I move my head away as a reflex action, to not be hit by the soundwaves.

I will hurt you more than a gunshot
that's only the beginning of what you deserve . . .

HE WAS STARING DIRECTLY AT HIM.

He always stared at him.

He never took his eyes off him.

Vittorio's father stared at his son for the duration of his visit. He had light blue eyes. So light they were almost grey. He kept his eyes wide open, as if he didn't even want to shut them to blink. They followed Vittorio's every move. From the moment he walked into the room behind his mother, to when he placed the fresh flowers in the vase and cleared the bathrobe off one of the chairs and took a seat, Vittorio's father never took his eyes off his son.

And he never said a word.

Not once.

He stared in silence.

His mother, no. She was never silent. She'd begin talking in the corridor with the nurse from the retirement home and when she entered the room she'd skip from one subject to the next with complete indifference, neither changing the tone of her voice nor the volume. She was talkative before, too: on the path that led to the villa, in the car, on the motorway, at home, during lunch, and earlier. She started talking the moment she woke up. In a way, it was as if she always talked to his father, even from a distance.

"Did you see Vittorio's come to visit? When did you see him

last? He said he's going to be at home for a while, so maybe he'll come back to see you again."

Sitting in the corner, with one arm resting on the table top, Vittorio reached out to touch a drop of water that had dripped from the rim of the vase. He didn't say anything either. He'd answer one of his mother's questions when she asked him something. He'd open his mouth, slowly and painfully, he'd mumble or whisper or try to begin sentences that he always left hanging, and when he felt like he'd put enough words together he'd stop talking and go back to being silent, observing the drop of water that he was squashing on the table, evaporating under his finger as he spoke.

His father had been at the Villa Maria di San Lazzaro retirement home for three years now. They took him there after the second time he wandered off and got lost. He had acute Alzheimer's. When they had found him in Trento after he'd gone missing for a week, and no-one knew how he had got there, his mother decided to put him into a retirement home in Villa Maria. There were too many dangers at home – the terrace, the door that she left open when she went out to do the shopping – and Vittorio was never there to help out. So, Villa Maria it was. But she went to visit him every day, sometimes even twice a day, and she always talked to him.

"You know that the Festa dell'Unità is much quieter now? Do you know that Pina's daughter is getting divorced? Do you know that signora Marangoni's daughter takes drugs?"

Vittorio did not look at his father.

He avoided looking at him whenever possible. Just stared off into the distance when he spoke and if their eyes met by chance, he immediately looked elsewhere, as if he had noticed something – a fly, his mother's sudden movements, something that required his attention, the drop of water on the table.

Rubbing his fingertips together, Vittorio wondered if his father was silent even when he or his mother weren't there. With the nurse, the doctor. Alone.

Silence.

He sat there on that powder-blue, 60s-style armchair, with its large rounded corners of fake leather, looking spectrally thin, hollow, enveloped in a robe that was too big for him, hunched over. His bony neck sank into his open-collared shirt, his thin wrists and ankles stuck out of the dark tunnels of his sleeves and trousers, his claw-like hands lay still on the armrests, his fingers were like gnarly dried up roots, the backs of his hands were covered with liver spots. His feet in his slippers were still, all day long. Day after day.

His father was only 55 but he looked as if he were a hundred.

Who knows what kind of silence exists in that head of his, Vittorio thought to himself. What kind of silence would it be? Maybe it buzzes, as silence does at times, filling up his ears from the outside, like a plug of wax. At first the buzz would be as thin as a veil, but then it would grow increasingly coarse, it would squeeze together and become a thick and compact curtain that squashes up against the tympanum, preventing any other noises from getting through. Silence like the sound of a swarm of wasps, a grating noise, incessant crickets and cicadas, the popping sound of boiling oil.

Or maybe it's a liquid silence, one of those black silences that builds up inside your head, at some imprecise point between your ears, like a miniscule dot, a small stain, an emptiness that slowly spreads, absorbing everything as it goes: tonalities frequencies vibrations timbres highs lows words sounds. Attracting them and swallowing them up in a leaden cascade: dense opaque obtuse; a black hole that expands, slips down the throat and eats up the heart lungs intestines; its only borders, the useless skin of the body.

Or maybe not. Maybe it's like a drop of water that's about to fall, that gathers itself at the apex of the cranium, inside the head, like water on a cave wall, that swells, stretches and then detaches itself, precipitating down the vertebral column, until it drips onto the seat of the chair, inside his trousers, in a tight, constant, precise drop. One drop after the other, a sharp, repetitive touch that vibrates subtly and hypnotically and, in so doing, gathers all sounds, blends them together and mixes them up. They slip down to the bottom and are nullified, the way a triangle in an orchestra keeps trying to make itself heard, until its sound is the only one left, its single drop of sound.

He realised that he was looking at his father with the same expression his father wore. Without thinking, he had shifted his gaze from no particular point in the bright empty room to his father's eyes, and the emptiness that was there had begun to fill up, they started to focus on everything. His father was staring at him, forcing himself not to blink. Something was going on behind those light grey eyes. Something so violent that it seemed to explode under the curve of the cornea. It was an intense and sharp and clear sentiment.

Terror.

For a moment, Vittorio had the sensation of loss that he felt whenever he experienced déjà vu, when the belief of having already lived something that he had never actually lived took away his breath, nearly fogging up his sight. But this wasn't déjà vu. Vittorio had lived a moment like this, years earlier. It was almost exactly like now. He recalled perfectly that expression of fear and terror in his father's eyes.

Distracted by the act of remembering which scratched the surface of his memory, Vittorio held his father's gaze for a fraction of a second longer than he would have wanted to. He continued to stare at him until the old man's head suddenly tipped back and his jaw fell open.

He couldn't talk. He could only sigh jaggedly, making sounds that got choked down the back of his throat in a sonorous gurgle, making his tongue stick out as if he was retching. Aborted words, words that collided against his teeth, words that slipped out in a short and muffled braying sound, more than a voice. His mother immediately stopped talking.

"Did he say something? Vincenzo, did you say something?"

Vittorio lowered his gaze in embarrassment and shut his eyes. His mother got up. When he opened his eyes she was standing next to his father, bent over him, her hands on his shoulders.

"What is it, Vincenzo? Do you want to tell me something? Oh God, Vincenzo, you've soiled yourself. Is that what you wanted to tell me? I'll change you now. Vittorio, would you leave the room for a minute please?"

Vittorio got up without looking back at his father. He let his eyes skim over the walls, taking in the useless objects around him. He nodded, sliding his chair back into place, under the table.

"Can you get home on your own? I was thinking I'd go and pick up Annalisa and go out with her."

"Of course I can, I always do . . . I'll take the bus. Vincenzo, Vittorio's leaving now, but he'll be back. You'll come back another time to see Papa, won't you?"

"Yes. I'll come back. Ciao."

THERE HAD BEEN DAYS, WHEN SHE WAS STATIONED IN Rome, when she didn't even wash her face. She'd just rub her eyes and drag her fingers through her hair. That was it. Those were days when there hadn't been time to do anything else – when she'd get up from her camp bed to take watch, or follow the suspect if he made a move, or changed apartments, cities or even countries, if their orders were such. Sometimes she didn't clean up even when she was at home, on holiday or on sick leave. But usually it was when there wasn't time.

Ever since she joined the Force, Grazia had to learn to live with many things. First of all, with odours: both hers and others', the smell of unwashed bodies, dirty hair, dirty clothes, dust, stale smoke, the greasy metal of guns. She had to learn to live with sounds: the hum of the sound equipment; the distorted voices of interceptors; the continual background noise of partners, colleagues who couldn't keep quiet, sniffles, coughs, farts – her own and others' – held back and not. At the Mobile Unit in Bologna things were easier, calmer.

But after four days without washing, a shower was more than a luxury, more than a necessity, it was a physical desire. A passionate desire. Inside the shower cabin, behind the frosted glass door, Grazia shut her eyes and turned the tap to the left. The jet of water came shooting down on her from above. The forceful rain fell on her body, cold at first, invigorating, then warm, then hot; she looked up at the shower head and let the water flow down her forehead, over her lips, through her hair. When she looked down and let the jet of water spray the nape of her neck and shoulders and back, she let out a moan of pleasure: true pleasure.

Just before she got out, when the skin on her fingers was wrinkled and almost sore from being under the shower for so long, Grazia filled her mouth with water and sprayed it against the tiles, like she had always done, ever since she was a girl.

She had wanted to wash so badly that she didn't even dry off. She passed her hands through her shiny hair, smoothed it back and squeezed it into a short, tight ponytail. She let the scented drops of water quiver on her skin until they evaporated. She left the bathroom naked and barefoot. Standing in the living room, in front of the staircase that led to their bedroom, was Simone.

She hadn't heard him come in. But after living together for more than two years she should have known that Simone always came home from the Istituto at this time. It shouldn't have surprised her, it shouldn't have made her gasp, but she had forgotten.

"Grazia?" Simone called out.

"Yes," she answered.

It was a useless question, formulated more out of surprise than anything else. Simone was blind. He had been blind since birth. Yet he was able to recognise Grazia from many things that had nothing to do with the simple act of seeing her. He wasn't even looking at her. He didn't even turn his head in her direction. He kept it turned to one side, his eyes were half closed. One eye was more open than the other, which gave his face an asymmetrical, almost crooked, look. He couldn't see her. But he heard her. He smelled her. He sensed her.

"I can't hear your clothes," he said. "You're naked."

"Yes."

"You just had a shower."

"Yes."

"Why don't you come over here?"

I don't know, Grazia wanted to reply, but she said nothing. She walked towards Simone and embraced him. The feeling of his warm clothes on her cool skin gave her a strange feeling. It was difficult to understand. As if the clothes bothered her, but she convinced herself that it wasn't that. Simone turned his head towards her and sought out her neck, grazing his lips along her shoulder. He breathed in deeply through his nose and pulled her close. Grazia stepped back, took his face between her hands and kissed him quickly. She pressed her lips against his until their teeth practically touched. It was a short kiss, intense, but too short. It didn't seem fake, but not really true either.

Simone took Grazia's hands off his face and moved quickly towards the coat rack on the wall, as if he could see it. He stopped just before bumping into it. He reached his hand out and felt along it until he had the brass hook in his hand. Then he took off his coat and hung it up, guiding it with both of his hands.

Grazia stood there naked and cool, smelling of shampoo and shower gel.

When she met him during an investigation in which he had been involved, Simone was a difficult and diffident young man. He used to spend his days in an attic room, listening to Chet Baker music and eavesdropping on mobile phone calls and police bulletins on his scanner. That's all he did: he never spoke to anyone, he never saw anyone, he stayed shut up in his attic, all alone. Then things had happened, the investigation came to an end, Grazia caught her man and Simone changed. He became better looking. Before, he barely even brushed his hair. He would just pull it back so it wouldn't go in his eyes. He never used to smile, he always grimaced. Now he had a good haircut, he listened to advice about clothing, he taught Italian at an institute for those with sight impairments. But his high level of sensitivity, the way he bowed his head when something bothered him, the way he stuck out his lip if something offended him, the way he couldn't hide anything, even when he was silent – that was still there. That's what Grazia had fallen in love with when she met him.

"Are you cold?" Simone asked. He heard her rub her arms with her hands.

"Yes, a little bit."

"Do you want to get dressed?"

"No."

Grazia moved towards Simone. She leaned up against his chest and pushed at him until he hugged her tightly, at which point she stood on the tips of her toes and kissed him, this time with a real kiss. Simone began to tremble. It always happened to him at moments like that: sometimes it was slight, other times, stronger. It wouldn't last long, but it had been that way ever since they first made love. Grazia remembered that first time and smiled as she kissed him. She sought out his tongue with her own, pressed up even closer and pulled him towards her by the shirt, leaning back against the armrest of the sofa and then falling back onto the sofa itself. Simone followed her, putting out his hands to feel where he was going. Grazia locked her hands behind his neck and pushed back against the armrest with her feet, sliding the two of them back over the cushions. Simone trembled harder, amazed by Grazia's scent, by her growing warmth, by her tongue – which moved over his lips – by her legs which moved up and around his hips. She slid back as far as she could, until she could no longer push against the armrest. With his arms wrapped around her, Grazia felt the full weight of his body and pulled him in closer, raising her chin so that he could kiss her neck. When Simone freed up one of his hands and touched her between her legs with the tips of his fingers, Grazia felt discomfort which she tried to hide by taking a deep breath. Simone might have noticed because he tried to pull away his hand, but she wouldn't let him. She pressed up against him and thought back to the first time he had ever touched her, when she had been sitting on his knee. She had guided those hands, the hands of a boy, under her shirt. She had liked that boy who couldn't see her, but who noticed her, the boy who told her she had a blue voice and blue hair, because blue was the colour of beautiful things. She had liked the way he sang "Summertime" when she got close to him, because it was from the advertisement for the deodorant that she wore. While she was thinking about that boy trembling in her arms, Grazia felt herself get warmer and wetter, and so she hurried and undid the belt on his trousers and pulled them down, a little roughly. She took him in her hand and guided him inside her, gritting her teeth for a moment. Suddenly Simone stopped trembling. He raised himself up, he wanted to kiss her, but she turned her head away. Instead, she took his hands and placed them on her breasts, pressing down on his fingers so that he would squeeze her. She held on to him, she kept her arms crossed behind his neck, her legs wrapped tightly around his thighs, her forehead pressed against his shoulder and her back curved to absorb his thrusts, one after another, curved, contracted and tight, faster and harder, until he came.

When Simone suddenly relaxed in Grazia's arms as if he had lost consciousness, she continued to hold him. She was afraid of looking at him in the face, she was afraid of seeing his expression. She didn't know how to pretend; she was scared that Simone knew it hadn't pleased her, that she had done it because she felt obliged to, so she kept him pressed up against her shoulder, her fingers in his hair, until he was the one who shook himself awake, practically shaking her off, wriggling free of her embrace. He shuffled off into the bathroom without saying a word, holding his trousers up by the belt.

Grazia shut her eyes. She sniffled a little, but quietly, so Simone wouldn't hear her. One tear, a single tear, rolled out of the corner of her eye, down her cheek and under her chin. Then she heard Simone swear out loud in anger from the bathroom. She sat up.

"What's the matter?" she asked from the doorway.

"You didn't put the shampoo back where it belongs." Simone said. Grazia went into the bathroom and picked up the bottle that was pouring down into the sink and screwed the cap back onto it.

"If you don't put it back each time you use it, I won't know where it is," Simone said. "Or I'll bump into it when I reach for the soap. You know how it is, Grazia."

"I know," Grazia said. "Sorry. I forgot."

"You've been very forgetful recently."

"It's because of work, Simo'. There's always trouble at work." Simone sighed.

"I didn't mean that. You go away for two weeks and you've already forgotten what we talked about. We talked about your work. I know that you're rarely here and you know that I miss you when you're not. But for some time now I miss you when you're here, too. Why, Grazia? Why is it like that?"

He pouted and Grazia shut her eyes so she wouldn't have to see him. She needed to sniffle again, but she didn't. The tears came rolling down her cheeks, but she waited until her voice was calm before she spoke.

"Come on, Simone," she said. "Let me wash up first, all right? I have to get back to the Questura. We can talk about it later."

Simone shrugged. He bent down to pick up his trousers and walked past without even touching her, as if he could see her.

WHY DO I SUDDENLY FEEL SO TIRED? I LIKE FEELING
her warmth on top of me but every time we're together, I
suddenly feel like I have to come up with an excuse that won't
offend her. That won't delude her. Why has it become so tiresome
all of a sudden?

"Ouch . . . what's that?"

Annalisa was kneeling on the passenger seat next to him. She
kept her arms wrapped tightly around his neck, as if she were
afraid he would get away from her. Vittorio took his gun out of its
holster and leaned forward to open the glove compartment. It was
hard to do because she wouldn't let go, but he managed to slip the
gun inside. He would have liked to turn down the radio, which
was playing very faintly, but the knob was too far away.

"Do you always have to carry that thing?"

"No . . . it's a habit. I forget I have it with me."

"Why do you need it? I'd feel better if you didn't carry it."

"Me too, but the insurance companies want me to. The
premiums for jewellery salesmen are already high enough."

"Would you ever use it? I mean, if you had to. Would you ever
shoot a man with it?"

Thought: the two men on the motorway, but never with this
gun and never just like that; there's always a right way of doing
things.

Another thought (a fleeting one, and for some reason in black-

and-white): his arm extended. Bang! The bullet exploding against the man's temple, his lip curling back, as if tasting something bitter. His head flopping to the side, his legs giving way, his arm extended. Another shot when he's down. Bang!

"No, I don't think so. But I can't say for sure."

"I don't think you would. You're not that type of person. If you ever get held up just give him all the samples – who cares?"

Annalisa moved over towards him. She hugged him tightly, raised herself up a little, passed over the brake and gear stick in one smooth movement and sat down sideways on his lap. She pushed him back against the seat and kissed him voraciously, with an open mouth, as if she wanted to eat his lips. Vittorio held her close and slid his hands along her smooth tights. He slipped his hands under her skirt and shirt, until he felt the elastic of her panties and the hot skin of her back. Thought: something distracted him, but he lost it and couldn't get it back.

The light from the streetlamps filtered through the leaves, shedding a dim glow on the shadows inside the car. It shone down on the edges of things, but didn't illuminate them. It made the grey, greyer and the black blacker; it added hints of blue. There was the sound of a deep trombone: it came through smokily, barely perceptible, and it was veiled by the intermittent tones of the bass.

"Do you desire me?"

Vittorio understood what distracted him. It was her accent. It was light, barely perceptible, hidden.

"Of course I desire you . . . can't you feel it?"

"But do you want me?"

"Of course I want you."

"But do you love me?"

Vittorio leaned forward and kissed her, letting Annalisa devour his mouth again. He slipped one hand inside her panties. The elastic from her tights was beginning to strangle his hand, but he reached down until he could feel the curve of her bottom and then further down still. Annalisa moaned and pressed up against him. Then, with agility and grace, shifted her position so that she was straddling him. Vittorio withdrew the hand that was under her shirt and reached around for the handle to move the seat.

Thought: what I'm missing is a little bit of an accent. But I need a stronger one than hers; I need an accent from Emilia Romagna, not from Bologna, that would be obvious, like the way she says *va bene*.

Thought: she holds back her *S* and her *L*. She has a lilt in her voice. I'll have to get her to talk more. A lot more. But afterwards, so I can hear it better.

The seat didn't go all the way back but it went far enough. Annalisa continued to kiss him, all the while moving and following his fingers. Then suddenly she stopped and took his wrist out from under her skirt. She slid over onto the passenger seat and Vittorio knew what he was supposed to do: he undid his belt and Annalisa took off a shoe, just one, and slipped her tights off one leg. She helped him take off his trousers and his boxers and then sat on top of him again: warmth and the rough white lace of her panties.

Vittorio looked at her: she was blonde and petite. Her eyes were closed. She bit her bottom lip. Annalisa was cute, but at moments like these she was beautiful. The shadows from the distant light fell over her face; they draped her in a sensual and mysterious expression. Her face was part-hidden by her hair, which had fallen over her eyes. She moved slowly, rubbing her body up against him, following the slow rhythm of the distant, smoky music. Now a woman's voice was singing. A hazy, distant voice. A woman who sang with a smile. Her voice went up and down as if she were trying to follow the irregular scales of the piano, but distractedly, without really paying attention to them.

Annalisa leaned forward over Vittorio without kissing him,

time enough to pull aside her panties. Then she moved towards him, hot and exposed, lifting herself up only for a second to take him in her hand and guide him into her.

Thought: I wish it would continue like this for ever; I wish it would end immediately.

Thought (confused): her accent, her accent, but I need one stronger than hers, afterwards I have to make her talk.

He put his hands under her skirt and held her hips, helping her move to the rhythm that she wanted. The woman's voice had become more raucous, grainier. It seemed that she didn't want to follow the sound of the piano any more, but rather that of the trombone that made itself heard every now and again. Even if the music was far away, even if it was different, he could tell that she was still smiling.

Thought: beautiful, beautiful, yes.

Thought: her accent. I need a broken nose, a porcelain barrel on a Heckler & Kock that's what I need.

Vittorio arched his back, and as he raised himself from the seat, the skin on his backside peeled away harshly from the upholstery, almost hurting him. He took his hands off Annalisa's hips and put them on her shoulders, following her movements.

Thought: when when now when right now can I come now wait when now when.

Thought: God I can't stop now.

Annalisa cried out and pushed down on Vittorio, taking his face in her hands and opening his mouth to kiss him. She continued to move on top of him even when he moaned, the muscles of his backside contracting and his back arching. He tried to resist; he tried to stay that way until it was no longer possible, but then he slipped out, damp and soft, squashed by the last thrust.

Annalisa kissed him again, lightly this time, tenderly, with a closed mouth. She slid back over to her seat. She wrapped her arms around his neck again and held him, her blonde head resting on his shoulder, until Vittorio started moving around because he was cold. He always felt a little ridiculous with his trousers down like that and his pants around his ankles. Annalisa opened the glove compartment and pulled out a packet of tissues. She wiped herself and passed one to Vittorio. Even before he had finished cleaning himself up, she was ready. She had put back on her tights, she had straightened her shirt over her chest and placed her glasses on the bridge of her nose. She gathered her hair up into a ponytail with a hair band that she had held between her teeth. It occurred to Vittorio that this was the way she looked when she was at work in the library in Ferrara: blonde and sexy in those thin glasses, her straight hair gathered in a smart ponytail. Elegant, provocative and intelligent, all at once.

The music on the radio had changed. The woman who had been singing with the trombone and piano was gone. Someone else had been talking: quiet, incomprehensible words in a low, monotonous voice. Then there had been another song, also seeming far away. It filtered out of the speakers and into the grey and blue interior in a whisper. You could tell this song was sad from the very first notes. Really sad.

His stomach hurt. Thought: all that water I'll have to drink tomorrow, all that water.

Thought: I have to get her to talk, listen to her speak.

Annalisa took off her second shoe and stretched her legs out over Vittorio who was busy fastening his belt. She took his hand and placed it on her thigh.

"Would you tell me why we always end up doing it in the car like two teenagers? You're 30 and I'm 29. I have an apartment all to myself here in Ferrara. But even so, after we go to see a film we always stop for a minute in a car park and 'bam'. Why?"

Thought (a fast one): it's the best place to do it, in the car, with keys in hand – there's a way out if someone comes towards you with a gun.

Vision (like lightning): the explosion of a gun being fired, blood spraying against the window, eyes rolled back: white white white.

"Maybe because in a way we still are children."

Annalisa nodded, suddenly serious. She rested one of her feet against the fly of his trousers and moved Vittorio's hand higher up her thigh, but it was only a gesture, distracted and unintentional.

"That's the trouble. We're like two children. We're not a couple. We're two single people who choose to spend time together."

"That's not true. I have to travel for work."

"I know but it would be different if . . ."

"If what, if we lived together?"

"No, that's not it. It's that . . ."

Annalisa always spoke softly, as if she breathed the words and held them in suspense on a subtle and long *m* sound, like a *meow*.

Thought: not like that, not like that. Gentle but up and down with a lilt, not like a Venetian, her *s* is thick, not like someone from Emilia Romagna but she has thick *l* sounds, almost double ones, like the accent in Ferrara.

"Hear it?"

Vittorio raised his head. He looked around and tipped his head to see out the window.

"Hear what?"

"The song on the radio."

Annalisa raised the volume. A little bit, just enough so that she could hear clearly.

"Do you remember this song? It was the theme song from the Commissario Maigret show on TV, with Gino Cervi. They show re-runs every so often. Can you hear the words?"

"No, what are they?"

"'Day after day, life drifts away.' Weird isn't it? That's exactly what I don't want to happen."

"Weird? What don't you want to happen?"

"I want all of this to have a sense. I want there to be a project, something that will happen, so that all this doesn't just drift away, day after day. You leave and when you come back we see each other, we make love and then you leave again."

"I work, you know. I have to travel."

"It's not that. It's not that you're never here, it's not that you never call me or that you always turn off your phone. It's . . . a kind of long term project. Something."

Vittorio bit his lip and looked outside. There must be wind, because the leaves on the trees were swaying, out of time with the music.

"But I have a project."

"You do?"

Thought: yes.

"And does this project involve me?"

Thought: no.

"Yes, it involves you."

Annalisa smiled and leaned forward to kiss him and his hand slipped involuntarily up her skirt to her underwear. Vittorio leaned forward to kiss her on the lips, but when her foot accidentally pressed into his stomach, it reminded him of all the water he'd have to drink the next day.

AFTERWARDS I ALWAYS FEEL LIKE SUCH A JERK. NOT because of it. Not because of the guilt complex that's associated with it, not because of the way they say that it'll make you go blind, that it makes Jesus cry or that it's disgusting at my age. Who really cares about any of that. It's how it happens that bothers me. And why.

I'm sitting on the sofa flicking through the channels on the TV. It's kind of a tense, neurotic flicking because the remote doesn't work very well. I have to push the rubber buttons with my nail three or four times before the channel changes, and sometimes I even have to open up the back and jiggle the batteries around. Then the channels change at the speed of a spray of bullets; I stop only when the remote stops working. I don't watch anything in particular. Actually I don't watch anything at all, except when suddenly I catch myself watching an info-mercial or a fortune teller or a soap opera and I don't even know why.

My friend Andrea wrote a short story about a sofa like the one we have. Every time the main character sat on the sofa and his skin came into contact with the leather, the sofa would excrete a hypnotic enzyme that prevented him from getting up. If a sofa like that ever existed, it would be this one. I don't know how long I've been ensconced in this wrinkled, scruffy, brown hug. Every so often the thought of getting up hits me – a short electric circuit that cuts through my nerves – but then it vanishes, leaving me more worn out than before. Instead I keep changing channels; I leap like a mountain goat from quiz shows to mini-series, I watch a 70s police drama like *La Polizia spara* or a *Pierino* film, with Bombolo and Cannavale, and when I suddenly realise what I'm watching, I decide to change channels. And that's when it happens.

The channel stops on MTV. There's a girl singing, a cute little blonde, someone like Britney Spears, who coos out a pop song for 15-year-olds. I don't really care about her or anything but while I'm fiddling with the remote I decide to watch a little and suddenly I realise that she's sitting the same way Kristine used to, with her legs up, her heels dangling over the edge of the chair and her knees pressed into her chest. She moves her feet with the rhythm of the music and looks at me through hair that's fallen over her eyes. She smiles at me – Kristine – and all of a sudden I feel a cold finger in my stomach, somewhere between my stomach and my heart. I remember how I moved close to her without saying a word. I lifted her face towards me and it felt like the first time I kissed her. Her lips were dry but very, very warm. That's the memory that comes back to me. It does something to me. I stare at the cute blonde. I watch her as she gets up and dances through that absurd set and then I realise that the jeans she's wearing are almost identical to the ones that Kristine had on that time: tight, with a low waist and bell bottoms. Kristine's were lighter, and they were a less well-known brand name. She was sure of herself. She was smooth and cool when she got up and rubbed against my leg. It was almost summer. I had Bermudas on. When I think about it, the feeling gets stronger, harder. It pushes against me, it gets caught in the elastic of my shorts, I have to slip a hand inside my trousers to make room for it, to free it from the painful tangle of pubic hair and fabric. I keep my hand there. I close my eyes and want to stay just like that, looking for Kristine. The feeling rips and pushes inside me. I find it. She's standing on her tiptoes, she wraps her arms around my neck, her lips are dry and warm, her tongue fast and insistent. I didn't know it would be like that. I loosen my belt, undo the first button on my trousers, raise the elastic of my boxers with my thumb, to make room for my wrist. I couldn't care less if Morbido comes in or if the rent lady comes in, or if I go blind or if Jesus weeps. I open my eyes for an instant to look for something of Kristine in the blonde; it's slipping away. It's getting away from me. I need something to hold on to before it becomes only a memory – a strong but useless one – and I find it in her mischievous smile, in the strange movements of her mouth. It makes me think of Kristine's lips. With that I flop face down on the sofa, my face buried in the smooth, wrinkled leather, and I stay there, breathing in the dust, until the end.

Then, naturally, I feel like a jerk. Partially because the video with the girl has ended and in its place is an advertisement for a new record by Gianni Morandi and it makes me feel stupid to see Gianni looking at me with that big smile of his. But I also feel stupid because I didn't want to do it. Believe me. I told myself I wouldn't do it any more, that I wouldn't find myself panting, cold and sticky, in this ferocious emptiness without Kristine, without her lips, without her heat pushing against my stomach and in my hand. I want to cry. All of a sudden I remember a film I saw when I was little, where there was a little boy who was crying desperately. I don't remember why he was crying. He was on a bed, face buried in the pillow and the voice-over said. "He cried himself to sleep." That's what I'd like to do. Cry myself to sleep.

Dog comes and nudges me out of my daydream. Maybe he smells something strange. He comes up to the sofa and sticks his face into my lowered trousers. I push him away, but inside me I feel a strange tickle that is both surprising and scary. He insists, so I stand up, pull up my trousers, arching my back so the sensitive part of my skin doesn't touch the zipper. I don't know what to do or where to go. Dog takes advantage of that. He hooks my knees with his paws and rubs his banana shaped head against my shin, his face against my thigh, eyes closed. It's as if he'd already fallen asleep. I feel ridiculous. And what's more, I'm desperate. Suddenly this feeling becomes intolerable. Not upsetting, painful, or ferocious. Intolerable.

"*Basta!*" I shout with all the voice I can muster. It comes out dryly, it reverberates like an explosion, and my vocal chords burn.

Dog moves away and flops back down on the floor. I quickly buckle my belt in case someone comes running in to see what the trouble is. No-one comes, not even Morbido who's in the next room, studying. The only one who seems to have heard me is Dog. He looks at me with a frightened expression in his eyes.

And then I feel terrible again. It's as if I shouted at Kristine, as if I was saying *basta* to my whole life, to everything that I am. And I don't want to say *basta* to Kristine. I realise that I have only two choices: either I throw myself down and cry until I fall asleep/die (which would be better); or I do something about it.

So I do something about it.

Ignoring the cold, sticky feeling on my stomach, I go into the corridor, where the telephone is. I'm supposed to note down the number on the meter so that I know how much I will have to pay for the call, especially because I'm calling a mobile phone, but I know I won't do it. Anyway, the numbers in the notebook and on the meter haven't corresponded for a long time.

I dial and wait. Finally, she answers.

"Hello, Luisa? I need your help. No, it's not what you think. I need your help with something."

THE MAN GETTING ON THE ESCALATOR NEAR THE check-in area at Malpensa International Airport looks like he's never encountered a moving staircase before. The girl at the information desk watches him gradually appear bit by bit on the marble horizon of the first floor. Gripping the handrail, shaky but determined, he watches as the toothy edges of the steps disappear into the iron grid. He's shaky but obstinate and resigned about getting over yet another hurdle. She watches him take a few stiff and limping steps and then stop, with a sigh of relief, on the marble floor. A woman pushes past him and a grimace of pain crosses his face. He must be 70. Or an old looking 60. Or a really old, really worn out 50. He reminds her of her grandfather, who used to be a steelworker in the Falck factories in Bergamo.

He's gripping a sheet of paper in his hand. He's not really reading it, more looking at it, as if it should be talking to him. She waves him over with her hand and waits patiently for him to arrive. Flight AZ 4875 for Frankfurt. Alitalia desks 25–32. Not at all, it's a pleasure. And she smiles, not the usual white parenthesis that she reserves for clients, but a real smile.

The girl at check-in desk number 27 watches him hobble up, one hand gripping the plastic carry-on travel bag that he has slung over his shoulder and chest, the other one gripping the handle of his suitcase, his backside sticking out. She's already got him worked out: he's eager, willing, ready to do everything he's asked, but awkward, bumbling, inexperienced. It must be his first time in an airport. No, you can't take that one on board with you. Place your suitcase on the belt: standing, flat, whatever way you want. Standing. No, all right, flat. Whichever way you like. No, no document is needed. Iberia would ask you for one, they have to, but Alitalia doesn't.

Why is she talking so much to this man? Usually she just tears off part of the ticket, makes her annotations, slips it into an envelope, asks the passenger if he wants a window or an aisle seat and that's it. She doesn't like her job. Why is she talking so much to this man? Maybe because he reminds her of her grandfather. But unlike her grandfather, who is tough and always confident, this man has a lost look about him that makes her feel tenderly towards him. As if she were the older one, as if she understood something about him. After she circles the gate number and the departure time on his ticket several times, she leans over and points out where he should go. Yes, over there, just around the corner. Yes, but not right away, wait for 15 minutes or so because they haven't opened up the gate yet.

The boy at the bar sees the man leave the check-in desk and knows immediately that he is going to come over to him. He sees him hesitate for a minute and let his gaze drift over the armchairs in the waiting area, which were all taken, and then he sees him look up and see the bar and smile. Sure, it might look different from the one he's used to. The one in his neighbourhood or his town probably doesn't resemble this black-and-green bar, with a neon banana hanging in the air above it, wedged in between the newspaper stands and the mobile phone vendor, but a bar is a bar. Even he, who'd only been working there for less than a year, knew that. He used to feel differently about bars: he used to go in them only for a coffee or a quick drink with his friends, but now, when he walked into a bar, he felt at home. But the man does something that surprises him. He had expected him to order a glass of white wine, a beer, or a coffee at least, but instead he orders a small bottle of water which he drinks in a hurry, filling up the plastic cup twice and drinking it immediately. He looks exhausted. When he finishes, he looks like he is in pain. He sighs, a wheezing sound coming from his broken nose.

The man walks into the guard's field of vision almost as soon as he leaves the till where he paid for his water. He wouldn't have noticed the stocky, stony old man with the limp if he hadn't walked directly towards the entrance area and then suddenly stopped, and begun rifling through his travel bag. The guard stops talking to his colleague, who is sitting at the monitor of the metal detector and watches the old man. He sees him pull out a manila envelope and then walk over towards the queue of Americans busily emptying their pockets into plastic baskets before going through the x-ray machine. The old man waits nervously for his turn. The guard steps away from his colleague's desk and walks over towards the old man, his hand raised, halting him. The old man had walked right through the x-ray machine without even removing his carry-on bag.

It is more the sudden appearance of the guard than the alarm that sounded on the x-ray machine that stops the old man in his tracks. He looks frightened and upset. The guard notices his embarrassment, he sees the way he cowers and turns around and bumps into an American behind him, looking up, looking around, not knowing what to do.

All right, all right, don't move. Step back. There, good. Now place your bag on the belt, like that. Now place all your metallic objects in this tray: keys, change, mobile phone. The guard glances quickly at the monitor, where the carry-on bag is being viewed by his colleague. Glasses, medicines, keys, a magazine, a small Swiss army knife, something that looks like a jumper. "Yes, your change goes in the tray, too, thank you. That's it, on the belt."

The alarm rings again. This time the man doesn't look scared.

He shakes his head and opens his arms wide, gesturing that it's not his fault, that it was inevitable. He stares at the guard and holds out the manila envelope. He starts to explain that his son said that it would happen. He says he's never been on an aeroplane before and doesn't really know how to do it. The guard takes the manila envelope, opens it and removes two x-rays and two sheets of thermal fax paper, one in Italian and one in German. He looks at the x-ray and sees clear and blurry shapes that look like an ankle and a foot. The man keeps talking, insistently though anxiously, explaining that his son lives in Germany. In Frankfurt. He's an engineer and this is his first visit to see him. He doesn't really know what to do. He has a metal pin in his leg after an accident at the steel factory, many years ago. He says his son was sure the alarm would go off; he himself wouldn't know as he's never been on a plane before.

The guard looks over the sheet of paper. It says "To whom it may concern . . ." and then everything that the old man is telling him in his open, slippery, singsong accent, with those thick *s* sounds, and the *l*s that seem to hook onto each other and stretch out, swollen and puffy. He puts everything back in the bag with a nod. "All right, go ahead, it's fine, every so often it happens, don't worry." He takes the magnetic wand that's resting on the table next to his colleague and waves it over and around the old man, who instinctively raises his arms above his head. It rings when it passes close to his right ankle, as it should. The guard hands him back his x-rays. He tells him he can take everything. He watches him pick up his keys and loose change and put them back in his pocket. It occurs to the guard that he'd like to ask the old man all sorts of questions, like how he broke his nose, if he had to put his arms up like that during the war, if he comes from Modena like his grandfather (who worked on the Motorway Police Force until he retired and who spoke almost exactly the same way), why he's going to visit his son on his own. Where his wife is. Whether she's still alive. But he doesn't ask any of this. He waits until the man has put his bag over his shoulder and chest. "You can go now." And then, even though he never does it, and even though he's not wearing his beret, the guard salutes the old man and watches him move off towards the gents.

Vittorio goes into the gents. He moves quickly into the last booth and closes the door. His bladder is bursting from all the water he's been drinking ever since the early hours of the morning, but he doesn't relieve himself. He would like to turn around so he isn't facing the toilet and won't be tempted to use it. But he needs to use it. He lowers the seat and lid and puts his right foot up on it. He takes off his right shoe and pulls down his sock. Tightly taped to his foot is the metal carriage of a Glock .40 calibre, with the barrel and the silencer. He cuts the tape with the Swiss army knife which he has extracted from his bag, without paying attention to the two deep, bruised grooves that the gun has cut into the skin of his ankle.

It's better that way, now I won't forget to limp.

He undoes the zip on his jacket, unbuttons his shirt and withdraws the rest of the Glock from the stuffing around his body. The drum, the handle and the magazine: all are made of plastic and as such were invisible to the airport metal detector. He connects the barrel to the drum and slides it through a few times, pushing down on the release on the left side of the automatic handgun to free up the breechblock, and then he squeezes the empty trigger twice. Raising his trouser leg up above his knee, he reaches for a row of bullets that are attached to his calf. He cuts through that tape with his knife too, slides off the magazine and fills it with the bullets, one after another.

Thought (a quick one): a porcelain barrel for a Heckler & Kock prototype is too hard to find.

Thought (very quick): even porcelain bullets aren't necessary; it's better this way.

He slides the breechblock through and brings the bullets into the barrel. He extends his right arm and closes one eye. Three white circles for taking aim: two on the sides, further back, and one at the centre, on the x that was formed by four tiles on the floor. He opens his eye again, lowers the barrel of the gun, raises his jacket and slides the gun into the back of his trousers, behind his belt.

When he leaves the gents he notices how much his foot hurts and realises that it really won't be difficult to remember to limp. In addition to his right shoe, which, unlike the left one, he had stuffed badly and too quickly, his bladder was driving him crazy. It was tugging as if it was going to explode, forcing him to keep his hips back and walk jaggedly. For a second he thought about going back into the bathroom to let out just a little bit, but he knew that then he wouldn't be able to stop. So he gritted his teeth because the Alitalia Business Class Lounge was still a way off, all the way on the other side of the duty free area, with its Calvin Klein shirts and Gucci belts.

The old man who is walking down the silent, empty corridor of the Malpensa airport seems to have acute prostate problems. He's limping and looking around. There's a look of pain on his face, which is highlighted by his broken nose. To Calazzo, who's sitting on the first chair in a row of cream-coloured armchairs, the man looks lost. There's nothing else at the end of this corridor except the door next to him leading to the Alitalia Business Class Lounge, which is for members only, or travellers in possession of a Magnifica class ticket, or members of parliament and other VIPs. This fellow doesn't look like he falls into any of those categories. On the contrary, he reminds Calazzo of his grandfather, who was a farmer in the countryside near Lecce. He'll probably turn around, Calazzo thought. He raises his arm to stop him, but is held back by his suit jacket, which is too tight for his big deltoids, and by his Beretta .92 in the holster under his armpit. He presses a finger to his ear; he's ready to call Bonetti, because this man isn't turning back. He's coming closer, as if he wants to talk to him.

He asks for directions to a toilet.

He doesn't know. Ordinarily he would have just said no. Actually, he wouldn't have said anything at all, he would just have shaken his curly head of gel-infused hair, but for this old man he leans forward and points down the corridor. "It's down there, back where you came from."

The man turns around with some discomfort and sighs heavily. "*Ostia*, oh Lord, all the way down there? I don't know if I can make it, I can't hold it any more. What's that door? There must be a toilet in there. Would you watch my bag for me, please?"

Calazzo would like to do several things, but the necessity to do them all at once means he can't manage any of them without difficulty. He looks at the bag on the armchair next to him, he presses his earphone into his ear, he pulls the microphone on the wire close to his mouth. "Bonetti," he says, then "No, wait a minute. You can't go in there."

The door opens and a man who doesn't look like he's supposed to be there limps into the business class lounge. Bonetti gets up from his leather armchair and has two simultaneous thoughts. Where the hell is Calazzo? and who is this man, Gepetto or something? He takes one step towards him when he sees the man being yanked back by Calazzo into the doorway, his mouth opening in surprise, pain and offence. Bonetti jumps forward and extends an arm to steady him before he loses his balance, and says, "Easy Cala', for God's sake. Take it easy, go back outside." With the other hand he motions to Rivalta, who has got up from his position halfway across the room, to stay where he is. He lets go of the man's arm. He's clenching his teeth in anger and breathing heavily through his broken nose. He nudges him back towards the door. "Terribly sorry, sir, I'm with the police. Ispettore Bonetti. Your ticket, please."

The woman in charge of the lounge steps out from behind her black glass desk. She's only 23, but she's in charge and lots of things are going on that she doesn't particularly like. She doesn't like the fact that the police took over the Club room so they could put that blond Russian man in there (he hasn't stopped serving himself drinks and pastries since he came in). She doesn't like it that the thin, balding inspector makes her telephone continually to find out how late the flight from Leningrad will be. And she really doesn't like the way they're treating this old gentleman. He could be her grandfather after all. So she walks up to them, her skirt swishing over her knees as she crosses the lounge, pushes aside the inspector and smiles at the old man. "Yes, what is it? Is there something I can help you with? Unfortunately this room is reserved for first class passengers only, sir. Do you have a ticket for Magnifica class?"

The man doesn't speak; he can't. He opens his mouth to mumble something and stretches out his arm towards the end of the room, leaving the gesture incomplete. The toilets are all the way on the other side of the room, the girl knows it. She is about to turn towards them too, instinctively, but then she stops herself because she sees the man's eyes. He's confused and stunned. She has never seen someone that age look so confused. It pains her. Then she lowers her gaze and sees the dark stain spreading across his pale trousers.

Bonetti takes a step back, as if he's afraid of being sprayed. The man covers his wet trousers with one hand, looks up and seems like he is about to cry. The girl grabs his arm and pulls him back inside the lounge. The toilet is over here, come with me, don't worry, we'll take care of everything.

Vittorio lets himself be guided to the end of the room, trying to control the relief that makes it easier for him to walk. When they reach the bathroom door he slips his hand into the back of his trousers and grabs his Glock.

Thought: first the bald guy, then the little guy, then the stupid one.

He turns around, puts his hand on the girl's neck and pushes her aside, towards Rivalta, who's sitting on an armchair with a magazine on his knees. He shoots Ispettore Bonetti twice, throwing him back against the wall. Vittorio twists around, not at all held back by the stuffing he is wearing, and shoots Rivalta twice, once in the chest and once in the throat, then he turns again, spreads his legs and brings his other hand up to the gun, holding it thumb over thumb, finger over finger. He's sure the third policeman is inexperienced enough to come running in at the first sounds of gunshot, so he aims at the door, about half a metre above the handle, because he remembers that the guard is tall, and shoots one two three shots.

The blond man.

Vittorio moves quickly, even though his shoes are too big. He breathes through his mouth. He can taste the bitter powder of gunshot. In his ears he hears the muffled echo of the explosion, but just barely over the bubbling frantic sound that comes from Rivalta, who's writhing in his chair, his hands clawing at his throat. The other sound, a sharp sound, a regular sound, like a bell, must be the girl screaming. He looks over at her before turning to the door. She's on her knees on the floor, unharmed, in a state of shock.

The blond man is on his feet, looking at him. His mouth is moving, but Vittorio can't hear what he is saying.

Thought: cotton in his ears would have made them suspicious; it would have been excessive; next time, maybe.

He aims at the blond man's mouth, the white circle on his moving tongue, like a mint sweet. One shot blows off the man's jaw, he fires another shot as the man falls to the ground, dragging the pastry cart with him; Vittorio lowers his arms and aims at the man's head.

Thought: nothing.

When he leaves the room, climbing over Calazzo's body, careful not to slip in the blood that is spreading out across the floor, the corridor is still deserted. There is no noise other than the girl's scream. At that point he walks away, sliding his gun into the back of his trousers, under his jacket, and leaving his carry-on bag on the chair outside the lounge.

"THEY THOUGHT THEY WOULD BE SAFE THERE, AND IN a way they were. There were three of them and they were secured in the lounge. They should have been the only ones to have a gun in that part of the airport. Almost safer than being at the police station."

"Shit."

"Shit is right . . . the short guy might make it. But he'll probably never be able to talk again. Can you imagine? A .40 calibre bullet in his throat."

"Shit."

"I know. Hey, don't you have anything else to say today? Only got one word? What's the problem? Your balls in a twist?"

"C'mon, Sarrina. Of course my balls are in a twist. I should be in Cuba now, eating camarones and smoking myself a nice little Montecristo."

"And screwing like there's no tomorrow. What's that girl's name?"

"Mariana."

"Are you going to marry her?"

"If I can bring her here, yes."

"You'd be making a big mistake."

"Look, we already talked about it, Sarri'. And I don't feel like talking about it any more."

Sarrina shrugged. "Go, you pain in the ass," he said, looking in the rear-view mirror and moving into the slow lane to leave room for the Mercedes that was flashing its full beams at him. "I wasn't talking to you," he added to Matera, who wasn't listening anyway, his elbow on the armrest, his hand at his breast pocket, fingering the tip of a cigar. He was looking out the window at the roads that extended beyond the Milano-Bologna motorway: damp and grey with the impending rainstorm. Sarrina caught sight of Grazia in the rear-view mirror, lying down on the back seat, and he peered around to see better.

"What's our bambina doing? Is she asleep?"

"No, I'm awake. I'm thinking."

"About who? A macho Cuban?"

"No, an Italian killer. Or at least, I think he's Italian."

Grazia sat up straight, reached her arms around the two headrests and knit her fingers together in the middle.

"We don't even know his nationality," she said. "We don't know anything about him. What do we have on him?"

"A bunch of eyewitnesses," Sarrina said.

"Which, assuming that our hunch is right and this was the same guy, are all useless," Matera added.

Grazia nodded. They had rushed up to Milan as soon as they found out what had happened at the airport, sure that this was their man, unwilling to accept the fact that an old man with prostate problems and a broken nose had killed four people. They had repeatedly interrogated each of the people who had been there: the Alitalia agents, the barman, the policeman at the security check. They even went to the hospital to see if Rivalta could tell them anything, but the doctor in charge had sent them away. All the reports basically said the same thing: on such and such a day, in the year 2000, so and so does swear that the following is true: I saw an old man who had prostate problems and a broken nose. Grazia spent a lot of time with the director of the Club lounge, but couldn't get much out of her. She had nothing to say about his voice, except that it was gruff and that he had a heavy accent, which was surely fake. His dialect wasn't from the area. If he had been trying to fake a Milanese accent she might have been able to tell if he was Sicilian, Roman or Emilian, but not if he was faking a Ferrarese accent. Grazia didn't learn anything about the man's build either: was he trim? out of shape? muscular? scrawny? He had been wearing too much padding to tell. What about his height? He was slightly hunched over because he was old and heavy. His proportions were distorted by memory, and her memory was blurred by fear. Only on the third try was Grazia able to have her act out the scene without breaking down in tears. He was between 1.75 and 1.80 metres tall. To this information they could add the results of the DNA test on the cigarette picked up off the ground in front of Barracu's house. A row of black lines on a white sheet. Result 1: genetic imprint. As unmistakable as fingerprints, but useless without something to compare it to. Result 2: Sex, Male. That was all.

"We do have his bag," Matera said. Grazia raised her head and glanced sideways. The old man's plastic travel bag was stuffed into a clear plastic bag. Rectangular, red and white, no brand name. Old. Taped to the bag was an inventory of its contents. It looked like a grocery list. After the lab in Milan examined it for fingerprints they had put everything back inside. Grazia had gone through hell to get the bag. The Direttore wasn't convinced: they had to bring in the judge of the Direzione Investigativa Autimafia (DIA) and ask him to give it to them as a personal favour.

"There's nothing there of interest," Sarrina said, slipping back into the fast lane, accelerating suddenly, coming right up behind the Mercedes that had just passed them and flashing his head-lights at him. "There are no prints on anything and our friend from the lab says that the bag looks as if it went through the washing machine."

"There might be a hair," said Matera, "or a bit of skin in the zip."

"There's not a damn thing there."

Grazia sat back in her seat. She would have liked to put her feet up but she had on her combat boots and didn't want to dirty the seat of the rental car. It was an unmarked car. They rented out a different one each time so that the felons under surveillance wouldn't recognise the number plate or the model. Though it wasn't so important to be incognito as they didn't even know who they should be hiding from.

She decided to sit up, like a proper young lady. She pulled down the armrest and leaned her elbow on it. She bit the inside of her cheek as was her habit when something perplexed her. Something wasn't right. She had a thought, but it came and went too quickly for her to put it into focus, and then it slipped away. Now it was only a feeling, an irritating feeling. Every second that passed made her more and more aware that she wouldn't be able to remember. She shouldn't force it. It was like when you can't remember an actor's name or something – thinking about it only makes it worse. It would be better just to change the subject and wait for the thought to come back on its own.

"We should analyse the mandates," she aloud, though practically to herself, mumbling, not worrying about being understood. "What do Jimmy Barracu and this Russian businessman that was being extradited have in common? Is the Mafia behind all of this? Ours? Or the Russian's? Is one *cosca* doing another a favour?

"We're almost out of petrol," Sarrina said. "Should we stop for a coffee?"

He indicated and pulled onto the sliproad that led to the motorway services. He passed a row of trucks that were parked on the outskirts of the car park and sped up to slide into a free space under a straw roof, stealing it from a Fiat Punto that had slowed down to let three children run across the tarmac in pursuit of a coach that was about to leave. When Sarrina got out of the car, he noticed that the Punto hadn't moved and that the driver was glaring at him, so he pulled out his red-and-white police baton and waved it until the car slipped into gear with an exasperated sigh and went to look for another place.

"You bastard," Matera said.

"Get out so I can lock the door," Sarrina said, slipping his key into the lock. "Now you can smoke that gasper."

"Sarri' you don't understand a damn thing about cigars. You don't smoke a cigar like this, just wandering around a car park."

Grazia got out of the car. She stood on her tiptoes and stretched her arms above her head, then remembered to straighten her long-sleeved T-shirt in the back to cover up her gun. She motioned to Sarrina to open up the car for a second and grabbed her jacket, which she tied around her hips, pressing the Beretta .92 in the holster into her back. Then she followed the men up the ramp into the café.

It was crowded inside. Everyone was cold, caught out by the sudden arrival of autumn and still wearing short sleeves.

"Coffee?" shouted Sarrina from the line at the till, and she nodded, then gestured over her shoulder that she was going to the toilet.

As she made her way around the cash machine and down the stairs, she realised that her man could be there. He could be anywhere. It was a thought that bothered her; it irritated her like a persistent tickle in the throat. Usually it wasn't like that. Usually she had a face to go by, like the man with the youngish face from Provenzano, or the one with the lurid face from Brusca, or that odd face in Aglieri; there was always a face to concentrate on. This time there was none. This time her man was anyman; anywhere between 20 and 70, he could be taller than 180 or shorter than 175. He could be anyone: the truck driver with the shorts, flip flops and yellow travel kit under his arm; the travelling salesman with the worn out jacket and wrinkled tie; or the bus driver in his blue shirt who was coming up the stairs, his hands still wet. It could be anyone. She had tried once before to catch a ghost without a face, the time she pursued the "Iguana" in Bologna. She had caught him and she'd do it again.

But the anxiety didn't pass even in the vestibule near the toilet, where there were only women. Her man couldn't be there. Grazia chose the last booth, as she always did, and locked the door. She pulled down her trousers and lowered her pants, pulling them away from her with one hand and being extremely careful that her gun didn't fall to the floor. Then she reached back and raised her shirt and her jacket with the other hand and lowered herself over the toilet being careful not to touch the dirty porcelain. There, in that uncomfortable position, the thought that had been nagging her returned.

Back at the counter, Sarrina and Matera were talking. Matera shook his head when Sarrina asked, "Do you have any idea how many Italian blockheads marry Cuban women?"

Grazia made her way through a group of children standing in front of the register. They were fans of some team. They all had scarves, T-shirts and hats of the same colour. One of them stepped in front of her, jumping and dancing, his hands in the air. She pushed him away, rudely, and he had to grab onto the newspaper rack so as not to fall. "Hey, honey, what's the matter, nervous or something? On the rag?"

"Your coffee's getting cold," Sarrina said when he saw her coming.

"Forget the coffee," Grazia said, "I thought of something."

"What?" Matera asked.

"The bag. And the stuff inside it. No prints, right?"

"Yeah, so what?" Sarrina said.

"We think he forgot that stupid bag, but what if that's not so?

What if he left it there on purpose? That's why he erased all the prints, because he knows we'll find the shitty thing."

"So?" Sarrina asked. He was holding the car keys in his hand. Grazia took them and ran off, before remembering that in order to exit she had to run through the whole service station: past the food market, the cheese display, the newspaper stand, there was even a video shop. Once she got to the car she rolled her sleeves down over her hands like gloves, unzipped the bag and pulled everything out.

If he had erased the prints it was because he wanted them to find something.

If he wanted them to find something it was because it had a meaning. One of the items had been put in the bag for a reason.

Old glasses in a worn leather case. Black frame, slight astigmatism.

A bunch of keys. Five of them, each one with a different plastic grip, a label which read BASEMENT tied to them with string. A brown v-neck jumper. Clean.

A magazine, *Diana Weapons*. It was a hunting magazine. A page corner was turned down near the end to mark an article.

"Pit bull, the most dangerous dog in the world."

Grazia looked at the pointed face of the dog in the centre of the page. It was such a large picture that it occupied a double-page spread, the centre fold of the magazine dissected the dog's face – it had one staple on its forehead and another under its mouth. But it was the eyes that were the most strange. They weren't lined up; they looked out of place and distant. Sharp and black. Shiny. As if they were laughing.

"What is it?" Matera asked when he got to the car.

"We have to get back to Bologna," Grazia said. "We have work to do."

She tried to sit back in her seat, when suddenly the face of the boy in the service station came to mind: "Hey, honey . . ." Her period: how long had it been? Once it was as regular as clockwork – she would know a week in advance that it was coming – but now it was different. Her period . . . She began counting on her fingers. She got so distracted that she didn't even realise that she had put her feet up and stamped the imprint of her boot on the new upholstery of the rental car.

SOMETIMES, THOUGHTS ARE ARTICULATED IN THE mind in the form of words. They weigh heavily on the tongue and won't exist until they are spoken aloud, until they are structured into discourse, shaped into verbs, nouns, adjectives, sounds. The tongue rests on the bottom of the jaw, the tip of it pressing against the teeth, touching the edge of the upper gum. The tongue may be still, but it's never really inert. It vibrates, twists and swells, not enough to form a sound but just enough so that the words ring through the head. Now I'll do this, I'll say, listen, first of all, then: shit, I have to buy a new shirt. They all have the same mute voice, always the same, silent, slightly gathered voice, held back by breath. The thoughts don't always come out flat and smooth, though. Sometimes the words trip over each other, they get caught on a repeated word, they ricochet off the bottom of the tongue and fly back in. They start again, shape new sentences and stop again, the repetition like a mantra. After a while, if they remain tangled, they become soporific, hypnotic; the thoughts melt. When everything works together, discourse unfolds towards the end, bouncing off the palate, instinctively. You know that you've really thought about something when, despite the fact that your lips are sealed and you haven't made a sound, your tongue is heavy and tired, back in your throat. That's what happens when you pray too.

Vittorio was driving. He never moved. He sat very still, moving in the fast lane, travelling at 110 km/hr. He kept his hands on the wheel, more leaning against it than holding it, and looked straight ahead. His eyes were drawn to a bluish patch in the sky ahead, but he kept his gaze on the road. A big hole shaped like a branch or a hand with its long fingers stretching up, charged with electric, luminous blue that poked a hole through the livid grey sky. If the sun were behind it, it would be liquid, too. It would be swollen and blue, like a drop of ink falling from an fountain pen.

On the motorway, everything that's important takes place in front of you, Vittorio thought. The driver can't look to the side, he can't turn his head and stare out the window. Everything that happens on the side is perceived through the corner of the eye. And everything there is equal. The crash barrier of grey cement: long, flat and compact like a wall. Concave strips of metal marked periodically with the reddish bump of reflectors. Squared hedges of green branches, wild with sick flowers. Rigid plastic: to the right of the passenger seat, to the left of his ear. The sky, meanwhile, and the road, the landscape: it's all in front, framed by the wide angle of the windscreen like a television scene without end. Sight leads off into infinity. Everything is in front of you. Even that which is behind you, above you, or squeezed into the rectangle of the rear-view mirror: you still need to be looking forward to see it.

Sometimes thoughts are illustrated by the mind as images, projected like a three dimensional film, like a moving hologram with no screen. Sight, smell and the other senses continue to work on the outside, registering actions and sensations, but behind the eyes, in that closed oval space between the temples and the nape of the neck, right there, under the cranium, that's where thoughts take shape. Sometimes they are guided, sometimes they are built on their own, like dreams. The images form and move – that woman, that man, that place. Noises, music and words exist even if they are not heard; they have odours and consistencies that reach the skin, provoking different reactions, real reactions.

When it happens, there is no turning back. They do not wind in a chronological sequence; nothing new happens, they repeat themselves eternally, identically. Or else nothing happens at all and the details rewind like a film reel, but then they start in again, they focus on details that fill up the screen, they deviate onto other faces, other bodies, other movements. That girl from Alitalia. She's cute, he thinks. She's walking next to him in her olive green skirt and blazer, she squeezes his arm. Her hand on his arm. Her white nails on his arm. Sensation: relief, calm. Yes. The olive green girl walking next to him. His hand on her face: her wet mouth, her teeth. The girl walking next to me, his hand on her face, pushing her away. The gun. Sensation: nothing.

When they rise out of nowhere, the images are called fantasies. When they've already happened, they're memories.

Vittorio took the next exit off the motorway. He veered away to the right, drove up the ramp and at the toll booth he went through the telepass lane. He didn't care if he left an electronic trace. On the contrary. He heard the first beep, then slowed down to make sure the bar raised. He almost had to come to a complete stop to let another car, which was coming from his left, go by. When the toll booth was already behind him and he was turning onto the motorway that led to the border, he thought about the phone call he had heard on the radio the night before. The caller had complained that the telepass lanes were never in the same place at all exits, forcing drivers to make last minute decisions once they could read the signs and to slalom around to get into the right lane. He was right, Vittorio thought.

Sometimes, thoughts come into existence, suddenly and without form. They appear in the dark of the mind like a bolt of heat in the night sky. Like a release of silent, atonal electricity. Like a lightning bolt without light: mute and blind, which leaves the sky as black as it was before and so quickly that it is impossible to understand where it began and where it ended. Some of these thoughts ignite sensations that explode violently, or else they are released, as slow as gas, as states of mind in which we suddenly find ourselves, without knowing from where they came or from what they were spawned. Others trigger connections, produce concepts, resolve problems. They get structured into images and words, they move forwards. And there are other thoughts that we have no perception of: they remain in the darkness of the mind, as if they never existed. Maybe there's a warehouse in there somewhere, deep inside. Maybe they get filed away inside the memory, or rather the traumas remain repressed in the unconscious.

Or maybe they simply become lost and never return.

Vittorio stopped at the border control. He parked his car, walked into the Guardie di Rocca and handed over his gun. He always did things according to the rules, without taking any useless risks. San Marino, despite its proximity, was, to all intents and purposes, a foreign state. It had its own rules and regulations.

It didn't take long for him to leave his gun at the Guardie di Rocca. They knew him there. Then he got back into his car and drove up the hill into town, one hairpin bend after the next. Along the way he stopped at five different banks, each time depositing the sum of 20,000 lire in cash, thinking how, in just one week's time, he would have to do it again after going to Switzerland to collect the second half of his payment. Once he got to the top of the hill, he drove around the main archway leading into town. He stopped in an empty square, got out of the car and went through an office door that was nestled between a bar and a newsagents kiosk. He glanced quickly at the pigeon hole labelled "Marchini Jewels", but there was only a coloured piece of paper there, an advertisement, which he ignored. The office was sparsely furnished. There was a table and a computer, a swivel chair and a file cabinet. In the next room were a toilet and two more cupboards. In one of them was a mop, a cleaning rag that was still wrapped in plastic, and a bottle of Mastro Lindo cleaning fluid. In the other was an Ithaca .12 calibre air rifle with a sawn off barrel, a precision semi-automatic Weatherby .30-378 with a Nightforce telescope with 36× enlargement and a Heckler & Kock machine gun, MP5, with a silencer.

Before leaving the office he took a spiral-bound notebook out of the desk drawer and looked at it quickly, running his finger down a list of names and numbers. He sighed when he read that this time he'd have to go to the Public Library in Cavriate, in the province of Bergamo, and he read the note next to the address.

Busiest time: Saturday afternoons (university students).

Pretty librarian. Nice, too. Would notice older users and good-looking men.

From the cupboard he took a dental prosthesis with a chipped tooth, a wig, coloured contact lenses and make-up to darken his skin. He chose some clothes: a pair of jeans, a white shirt, a blue jumper. He placed everything in his bag, looked at his watch and hurried out the door. He still had to retrieve his gun from the police station, find a place to change his clothes and drive all the way to Bergamo in time for his appointment in the chat room.

DING!

"They're back."

I've activated a program that tells me each time a certain username comes into the chat room. I did it on my own, without Luisa's help. Now every time PitBull or OldMan go into the chat room my computer goes "ding!" and lets me know. It could also go "ka-booom!" but I'd have to ask Luisa how to make that happen and I don't want to ask for too much. She's already helped me a lot.

Together we checked how many times PitBull and OldMan have met in a chat room over the past year. Fourteen times. Only fourteen. Then we checked to see how many times they were connected simultaneously. Fourteen. And never for more than ten minutes. PitBull and OldMan connect to communicate with each other and they don't even say very much. "Why don't they just pick up the phone?" Luisa asked, and I think that's when she became interested in the whole story, too.

We tried to find out something about them: where they connected from, for example. If they had been users in our area, we would have been able to see their phone numbers. But they were external users and they could have been connecting from anywhere, even Australia.

"They're back, Luisa, come and see."

Luisa gets up from her terminal and comes over to mine. She

does it in such a hurry that she forgets about Dog and climbs over him as if he were a bag. He doesn't even move; he goes on sleeping, his nose against the floor, making a big wet spot that enlarges with every breath he takes.

"Shit . . . it is them."

External users. I was lost by that point, but not Luisa. She knows more about these things, not as much as Mauri, but more than me. She had asked me why I was interested. Whether it had anything to do with Kristine, seeing that there was nothing else that interested me. A little bit, I told her. It's something I want to do. Something I can do. It's the only chance I have for escaping my own apathy, Luisa. Help me.

OldMan: Did it go all right?

PitBull: Fine.

OldMan: Here, too. Everybody's glad. Are you all right?

PitBull: I'm fine. As always.

OldMan: I'm not. I think I'm getting the flu.

Luisa leans on my shoulder to see the screen better. I feel her breasts against my back and I sit up a little. She doesn't even notice.

"Why don't they call each other?" she asks. "For what little they have to say. Why all the bother?"

External users. Luisa checked and managed to get the IP address of both PitBull and OldMan. A long sequence of eleven-digit numbers, divided in four groups, separated by a dot, 194.242.155.63, 195.321.192.34, etc. in which the first grouping indicates the provider and the last one the connected user. Independently, they don't mean a thing, because they always get adopted by different users, according to the availability at that moment. Shit.

PitBull: When's the next time?

OldMan: Soon. I have a client who's breathing down my neck.

PitBull: No problem.

OldMan: Even so soon?

PitBull: No problem.

Luisa shakes her head. She jiggles her foot back and forth and then jumps a little because she feels Dog's short, bristly hair. She comes around to my other side and leans on me as before, her arm on my shoulder, her breasts against my shoulder blades, eyes on the monitor. She's holding a lit cigarette and the smoke is making my eyes burn.

External user. Luisa said there was a way of finding out more about the user. It wasn't easy, but there was a way.

"How do you mean?" I asked her.

"Tell me why you want to know," she said.

"It's not easy to explain. There's no real reason for it. It's like when you're in love with a girl and she leaves you and you feel like shit and you can't think about anything except her, about how beautiful she was, how sweet she was, how much you miss her now that she's no longer there. Then you start thinking that it's not because of her that you feel like shit, but because you really are shit and that life is like that. At that point you have two choices. Either you wallow in it and you go on crying day after day and do things like watch MTV and . . . well, anyway, you stay there, doing nothing, day after day. Or else you break out of your apathy and you do something, anything, it's enough that it has any vague connection with her. You have to think about her to get going. Kristine loved a dog that looked like a pit bull. These guys are talking about pit bulls and they're doing it in a way that is strange and creepy and, shit, what do I know, Kristine wouldn't have liked it. I want to find out what's underneath. I want to do something that doesn't make me look like an idiot in her eyes, even if she'll never find out. I don't know if that makes sense, but that's the way it is. Is that enough?" At that point, Luisa smirked and explained how we could find out more about PitBull.

"External users. First you determine who the provider is from the first few numbers of the IP address and you call them and ask them who was connected on that day, at that time, at that second, with that IP. They know. They know the phone numbers of the users. The hardest thing is actually getting them to tell you."

Luisa's good at this. Better than me. She worked out a list of providers and called them from the office. With some we had a professional relationship, so they were easier. With others we had to come up with some kind of excuse, like that there was a user who had made a mess of things and we had to work out what happened, thank you very much. Some of the people wanted to call us back to make sure that we were an actual provider. Some of them didn't argue with us at all. As soon as we had the phone numbers we called 1412 on Telecom to get to the addresses.

"Welcome to Telecom Italia. This service provides the name and address for a particular telephone number. Please dial the telephone number you would like information about now."

We tried six of them.

PitBull: Public Library in Villa Spada, Bologna. Public Library in Varese. Cybercafé Andromeda in Padova.

OldMan: Leonardo da Vinci Airport, Fiumicino. Cybercaf' Xenia, Rome. Public Library Sabaudia, Latina.

All public places, usable by anyone. Useless.

We didn't even look at the other eight.

OldMan: This client has very specific requirements. It will be a difficult meeting.

PitBull: No problem. Just let me know when.

[Saturday, September 30, 16:08:52 Pdt 2000] PitBull leaves private chat room.

Luisa moves away from me. She sighs. She mumbles – fuck – and she goes back to her terminal and sits down. But she goes on staring at my screen. I disconnect and exit the chat room; my mind is elsewhere. OldMan said something, a word that explained everything. And that scares me. I'm thinking about two things. The first:

"Luisa, you know what these two bastards are talking about?"

"About dogs," she says.

"Yes, but not to sell them. There's something underneath it all, something horrible."

"What?"

"Dogfights. Did you see what OldMan said? He said 'It will be a difficult meeting . . .' a meeting between pit bulls, Luisa. Ferocious dog fights. They organise them."

"What bastards."

The second.

"Luisa, if they connect from public places it's useless, right?"

"Yeah, you saw the way it is."

"The old man said he was getting the flu, maybe for once he dialled up from home."

Luisa bit her lip and raised an eyebrow. Just one. I don't know how she does it. She has a pencil in her hand and taps it against her mouth, nodding.

"Could be," she says. She gets up from her terminal and comes over to mine. This time Dog raises his head, but she ignores him. She gets OldMan's IP.

192.204.197.12

It's a provider in Sabaudia, in the province of Latina. Luisa grabs the telephone from the table next to the computer and dials the provider's number.

She talks for a long time, some of the time to get the number, but mostly to shake off the guy at the other end, who from his voice sounded particularly sleazy.

She writes down the number on a piece of paper, but then suddenly grabs it away. She wants to do the 1412.

"The number you entered corresponds to . . ."

Surname and title: D'Orrico, Avvocato.

Christian name: Alberto

Address: Lungomare Sud, 25/a 04016 Sabaudia, province of Latina.

"There!" Luisa says with a smile.

I've never seen her smile before. I reach out and instinctively hug her. She looks at me strangely, surprised and diffident. But then everything falls apart again.

Not because of her, not because of her reaction . . . if she had continued smiling I probably would have kissed her. I don't know what kind of kiss it would have been, it would have been nice but not important. And afterwards she probably would have killed me. It's that suddenly I realise that none of this matters. What I wanted to do has been and gone and I'm screwed anyway. I got away from it for just a moment, for just one moment, and now here I am in the thick of it again. In a minute's time I will begin thinking of Kristine again, how much I miss her, and what a shit I am. One shitty day after another.

Luisa, on the other hand, seems euphoric. She calms down as soon as I let go of the paper on which she has written down the name, number and address.

"What do we do next?" she asks. I shrug.

"Hmm." She bites her lip, wondering. "I don't think we can go to the police. What we're doing is not exactly legal. And if they find out, we'll both get fired."

"Who knows," I say. "Maybe there's a helpline for dogs . . ."

"Let's think about it," Luisa says, getting up from the terminal and picking up the phone. "I have a friend who works at a dog shelter, as soon as I see him I'll tell him. In the meantime . . ." she slides the paper under the mousemat, so that the number is still visible and dials it.

He answers on the second ring, as if he had only just put down the receiver and was still close to the phone.

"Avvocato D'Orrico?" she asks.

"Yes."

"We know what you're up to, you bastard."

And she hangs up. She looks at me with satisfaction, takes another cigarette from the packet and lights it.

"We have to do something to get him worried," she says. "At least a little bit."

From: a.dorrico@hotmail.com
To: pitbull@libero.it
Subject: urgent!

Contact me for a new appointment. We have a problem.

GRAZIA'S OFFICE.

A temporary space on the first floor of the Mobile Unit that once was a storage room for archives. Now, stacks of cardboard boxes filled with cream-coloured files held together with a string were piled up against one wall, under the window.

Ten metres square. Two tables, one swivel chair, an armchair, a camp bed, a coat rack, a door, a window. Luxury items: a large magnetic message board and a rubbish bin.

On the grey plastic table in the centre of the room was a laptop: open, turned on, the glow of a dark screensaver (asteroids exploding into space). An external modem was connected to the Internet by way of a green plastic extension cord that disappeared behind the half-closed door. A mouse on a mousemat that depicted a hyper-real picture of a fried egg. Next to the computer was a mess of witness reports – more or less all of them of a general nature and needing to be read. Those that had already been read were face down and those still waiting their turn were in a pile (on the top one, in one of the corners, the brown ring left by a cup of coffee). Next to that pile were two very thick folders, both open. The first one was entitled "Barracu Murder". The second: "Akunin Murder". Under the cover of the second one, sticking out and upside down, was a black-and-white photograph of Ispettore Bonetti (a blood stain running down the wall behind him, all the way down to his head, which lay flopped over one shoulder; his eyes partially closed, one side of his nose encrusted with blood, the corner of his mouth open, showing his teeth).

On the table against the wall are the lab results on the bag found at the airport (negative), the report of the Direzione Distrettuale Antimafia on the possible connections between the Barracu and Akunin murders (none), a report from the DIA of Palermo on the Madonia Carmelo clan, which provided the mandate for the Barracu murder, and which details the search for known killers (none), handwritten notes by Di Cara ("none of the known killers is our man. I'd walk through fire on it"), a report by the DIA of Rome on Zruov Dimitri, the key mandate for the murder of Akunin, in order to distinguish elements similar to the airport killer (none).

In the rubbish bin: one plastic coffee cup.

In the pocket of the bomber jacket hanging from the back of the chair: a receipt from the pharmacy on via Marconi and a pregnancy test, still sealed in its box.

Grazia checks her first intuition. The computer she found in Jimmy's bedroom (belonging to the Barracu family, with both his and his wife's fingerprints on it) was connected to a site dedicated to dogs (http://www.dogfighter.com), and was open at an image of a pit bull terrier. In the magazine in the bag found at the airport, another pit bull stared out at them. Two coincidences indicate a connection: in a serial murder case this would count as a signature. How many other murders had been committed in the last few years where a pit bull was somehow present? Put in a request for information to the central archives of the Polizia di Stato. Send a formal request to UACV, the Unit for the Analysis of Crimes of Violence, with its computerised archives of murders without motive. Send photograms to laboratories in the provinces, to the Questure and to the Carabinieri offices.

Four answers.

Grazia's office. On the camp bed: a gym bag with a change of underwear, a jumper and a toothbrush. The first night she spent at home she and Simone didn't talk, they slept back to back, far away from each other in a bed that seemed far too narrow. (Where are you going with that bag? I'll be away a few days, for work, as usual. Will you come back?)

On the table against the wall, stacked up next to each other, were files with reports and information from:

DECEMBER 1999. PANDELLA MURDER, PERUGIA. At approximately 07:30 Professor Emilia Pandella left his house to go to work at the Silvestrini hospital, as he did every morning. He got in his car, which was parked at the side of the road, and had just started the engine when he was approached by a heavy-set man with a limp in his left leg. The man fired three rounds from a .40 calibre Sw into his head, killing him instantly. Successive eye-witness reports indicated that three suspicious individuals had been in the immediate vicinity observing the movements of the professor in the days leading up to the crime. One of them had been wearing a T-shirt printed with a pit bull logo, visible under the bomber jacket which the man kept open, despite the cold weather (Sm Perugia, Ispettore Gusberti).

JUNE 1998. D'ANGELO MURDERS – CABONA, ROME. At precisely 19:45 Cavaliere Francesco D'Angelo and his bodyguard Antonio Cabona, aka Nino, were gunned down by a round of automatic machine-gun fire, .9 calibre, as they stood inside a gated lift, heading towards the fourth floor of a building on via Beato Angelico, where the Cavaliere resided. Shooting from the second floor landing of the building was one Persichetti Elio, a so-called friend of the family, who lived on that floor and who was actually on a free holiday in the Maldives at the time. Elio Persichetti, who offered false information about himself and who disappeared after the murder, is described as an older man, with greying hair, a ruddy face and an apparently homosexual manner. He had already been seen in the environs on the days preceding the murder because of the constant barking of a dog in his apartment, which he declared was a pit bull (Commando Provinciale C C Roma, Capt. Lojaco).

MARCH 1998. RAVARRINO MURDER, LOCATION RESERVED. At 16:18 Maurizia Ravarrino, the wife of the Camorra boss, Michele Ravarrino, aka Biondolillo, was shot in the head by a gunshot .30-387 calibre. Signora Ravarrino had been hidden in a farmhouse in a secret location as she was involved in collaborating with the police following the death of her husband. The shot came from a nearby construction site and in all probability was fired from a precision weapon, given the distance (1095 metres). On the days preceding, and on the same day of the murder, the surrounding area had been thoroughly searched and secured by bodyguards from the Head Office and by the local Questura. Witness protection agency of Rome and the local Questura – Ispettore Supplementare Mattei Noted on the report, in Matera's hand-writing, was: "You were right. I had them do a Pattix with reports from all the guards. On the morning of the murder a tourist was stopped in a rented Renault Mégane Scenic. The guard didn't mention it to his colleagues because it was going in the other direction and because it stopped shortly after at Fontanafredda, Grosseto. Our friend must have walked back 15 kilometres to the villa without being seen. Why do I think it's him? Because the Mégane had a sticker on the rear window, and guess what was on it? A pit bull."

On the table by the computer, near the mouse, lay Grazia's mobile phone. It buzzed quietly, on vibrate. She didn't answer it, but she checked her voicemail. It was Sarrina: 'I'm in Como. I checked on the tip. In 1990 looks like our man Pit Bull killed a colonello in the Air Force who was linked to Secret Services. No-one wants to talk about it though. What should I do, look for the Brigadiere Carrone who filed the report?"

In the rubbish bin: four plastic coffee cups.

In the centre of the message board was the photograph of a pit bull cut out of a newspaper. It was surrounded by Post-its scrawled with notes. 1) Male, 175/180cm. 2) Professional killer, *not* a serial killer. 3) Good with weapons. Where does he train? Where does he get them? Check. 4) Skilled in the art of disguise. Where did he learn? 5) Milano-Roma-Grosseto-Bologna-Perugia-Como. All over Italy. How does he move? 6) How does he contact the clients? 7) How does he get paid? 8) Where does he hide out? 9) Who is he?

Grazia checked on her second intuition. To kill Jimmy and the others he used a glass bullet coated with plastic. They are difficult to use and to find. Have there been other murders with that kind of bullet? Send urgent photograms to all the Questure, Laboratories, UACV and Carbinieri Headquarters. Last minute idea: check both unresolved and resolved murder cases – and suicides, too.

Two replies.

Grazia's office: on the camp bed are opened files and folders, papers (verbal reports, technical surveys, optical reports, ballistic reports). Underneath the bed is a pair of black combat boots (kicked there in anger). The room is stuffy and smells of sweat.

On the table next to the computer is an autopsy report and photographs of Avvocato Bracchetti, Como. Next to it is a McDonald's wrapper with the residue of ketchup (McBacon + fries + 9 Chicken McNuggets), a box from Spizzico Pizza (tomato and mozzarella calzone), plastic containers from Great Wall take-away (Cantonese Rice, chicken with bamboo and mushrooms).

On the table against the wall, on top of all the other papers are two files:

SEPTEMBER 1998. PALADINO MURDER, FERRARA. A bank director was shot in the head three times while waiting for judgment on money laundering and fraud. Wax bullets, probably frozen with dry ice before being used. No ballistic report possible.

DECEMBER 1997. GRAZIANI SUICIDE. Woman fires one shot at her temple with a .22 rifle belonging to one of her sons. She uses a glass bullet coated with plastic. Explodes on impact. No ballistic report possible.

In the rubbish: wadded up pieces of paper with Post-it notes, 13 plastic coffee cups.

On the message board: the picture of the pit bull in the centre. Additional Post-its are spread out in a second tier. 10) Why would a professional killer leave his signature like a serial killer? 11) Bologna, Ferrara, Reggio Emilia. Untraceable bullets. (Second Post-it: stuck to the corner of the first). All of them are in this region. Why?

The mobile phone rings. It's on the floor, under the table. Vibration. She ignores it. Another message from Sarrina: "Why aren't you answering? I can't find this Brigadiere Carrone. It's as if he's disappeared into thin air. Should I keep looking?"

Grazia is sitting on the swivel chair in her office, her legs stretched out on the table, her ankles crossed one over the other. One sports sock hangs wispily from her foot. Her chin is lowered, touching her chest, her head resting against one of her shoulders. The tendons in her neck, on the left, are anaesthetised by sleep and will hurt her when she wakes up.

In the pocket of her bomber jacket is the pregnancy test. Still sealed.

"I TALKED TO MY FRIEND WHO WORKS AT THE KENNELS."

"Yeah, and . . . ?"

"You really don't care, do you? Anyway, he said that we should tell the police. I don't know, though. Maybe it's not such a good idea."

"No? No, you're right. Of course not."

"If we make an anonymous phone call, they're not going to take us seriously. I think we should stop it all right now. At the very most we can call this Avvocato D'Orrico back and scare him a bit more."

I mumble something in reply and shrug. I'm walking with Luisa under the porticoes of Piazza Santo Stefano. She's wheeling her bicycle and I'm walking alongside her. Every so often my ankle bumps into the pedal, but I don't care.

"Listen," I say to her, "I'm not coming in to work today."

"You're crazy, why not?"

"I have to study. I have an exam soon."

"Yeah, sure, as if I believe that."

"No, listen . . . I don't feel well. I'm sick."

"I don't believe that either. Why don't you just say you don't want to? I'm not the boss. I'm not going to fire you."

I'd kind of like to be fired. Not to have to work, not to have to do anything. I'd throw myself down on the sofa and sleep, or die of hunger or thirst. For a minute I feel a sensation of relief that loosens my shoulders and curves my back, making my arms hang down loosely by my sides. Then the anguish cuts off my breath, like a hand around my throat.

"You can stay home any other day, but not today. Someone called from the main office in Milan yesterday and asked if we were all going to be in today. I guess they're doing some kind of check, so the boss wants everyone there. Any other day would be fine. He'd get over it. But not today."

And when will I get over it? The other day I took a book from Morbido's room. He's taking a psychiatry exam and on his table there was this big, heavy, square, burgundy-coloured book: *Mini Dsm-IV. Manual of Statistical Diagnoses*. All of the mental illnesses categorised by symptom. I sat on his bed and flipped through it, looking for mine. Mood swings. Episodes of depression. Are five or more symptoms present simultaneously during a period of two weeks?

1) Depressed for most of the day, almost every day (yes).
2) A marked loss of interest or pleasure in all or most activities for most of the day, almost every day (yes, every day).
3) Significant weight loss without dieting, or significant weight gain (yes, loss of weight, not that I wasn't skinny before).
4) Insomnia or hypersomnia almost every day (yes).
5) Agitation or marked slowing down of psychomotor skills every day (yes).
6) Fatigue or lack of energy almost every day (shit, yes!).
7) Sensations of insecurity or excessive guilt or inappropriate behaviour, which could be considered delirious (maybe not delirious, but yes).
8) Reduced capacity to think or concentrate, or general ambivalence (I've always had that . . . just one more left).
9) Recurrent thoughts of death and/or suicide without a specific plan (hurrah! nine out of nine! I have them all).

When Morbido came back I told him.

"Morbido, you can use me as a case study. I am a perfect example of a major depressive episode."

"Fuck off," he said, "You're just an unlucky guy with a shitty life right now."

"Congratulations, Dottore Morbidelli, you have a true future as a psychiatrist. What are you specialising in?"

"Orthopaedics."

"Well, that's a relief."

I rub a hand across my face and realise that I haven't shaved in a long time. Usually you don't notice it because I'm blond, but it's been at least five days and you'd notice it on anyone. More than being bushy, it's a flat beard, bristly and sharp; as soon as it starts to grow it begins to bother me because it rubs on the collar of my shirt. For a moment I think about going home to shave and suddenly a wave of fatigue overtakes me and I know I won't. More or less this is what happens when I think about showering, too.

Luisa, on the other hand, has a fresh, clean smell. When she stops to cross the piazza I get close enough to her to recognise the smell of her shampoo, it's the kind that's made with the protein from Japanese silk. I used to use it too. Before. She's wearing a red wool zip-up cardigan with deep pockets. A packet of smokes is sticking out of one of them. She's also wearing an array of necklaces – African, Indian, grungy – and multi-pocketed army trousers and sandals. I look at her for a long time, taking advantage of the fact that I am behind her and that she can't see me.

We walk into the building where Freeskynet is located and Luisa locks up her bike in the foyer. When she bends down to lock up the front wheel with the chain her jumper goes up and shows her back. I wonder if I'm looking at her too much. I feel a twinge of desire and a lot of guilt, as in point number 7, above.

"Where's the beast?" she asks, on her way up the stairs. I get the

feeling she's getting used to him and that she's almost upset I
didn't bring him with me.

"At home," I say. "Shut in my room."

"He'll bark and chew your slippers."

"He'll just bark. He's already chewed the slippers."

We get to the second floor. We walk in. The boss is sitting
behind the desk where the secretary usually sits. He's filling out a
subscription form and looks pretty pissed off. "Good thing I said
I wanted everyone here," he barks.

"We're here," Luisa said.

"And you're late. Mauri and Christine still aren't here. And I
have to work as a secretary today."

At least he's doing something, I think to myself and I'm sure
Luisa is thinking the same thing because she looks at me and
smiles. I feel a touch of tenderness and then another heap of guilty
feelings.

Sitting in front of my terminal I experience numbers 2, 6 and 8.
I convince myself of two things: a) it will be hell to spend the day
looking at a monitor that I don't even have the strength to turn on
and b) Morbido is a real dick. I turn towards Luisa, who has got
settled into her chair, turned on her PC, undone the laces of her
sandals and lit herself a cigarette.

"Listen, Luisa," I start to say. "In your opinion . . . would it be
stupid . . . for me to go to a psychiatrist?"

"Because of her, you mean?"

"No . . . I mean, yes. Well, not just because of her. I'm afraid I'm
depressed."

I must have said it in a very serious tone because Luisa turns
and looks at me with a little frown line between her eyebrows.
She shrugs and hits a couple of keys, and then looks at her
monitor.

"Why?" she says. "Better to go to a psychiatrist than an
astrologist. I went to one, once."

She hits a few more keys and then waits. I look at her in silence. She knows I'm looking at her. In the end I give in.

"Why?"

"Eating problems. I weighed almost 80 kilos."

"And are you cured?"

She looks at me, twisting around on her chair. She grabs her jumper and pulls it up slightly.

"Look at me!" she says. "I now weigh 52 kilos. Of course I'm cured. It was three years ago."

I can't imagine Luisa fat. I can't imagine her sick, either. Pissed off, malicious, tough, problematic, yes. But suffering from an eating disorder, no.

"Why?" I ask.

"Why, what? Why did I get better? Because I followed a course of therapy with Dottore Vicentini."

"No, c'mon. Why were you sick?"

Luisa goes back to her terminal. She doesn't want to tell me. Or maybe she does. She wants to tell me, or maybe not me in particular, but she wants to say it, only she doesn't feel like it. Or rather, she feels like it but it's not easy.

"Did a guy leave you?"

Luisa smiles. First she smiles and laughs a little through her nose and then she laughs harder and shuts her eyes. I knew it was bollocks and I said it on purpose, to loosen things up a little, to break the ice. Why didn't I ever have thoughts like these with Kristine? I never said one sentence right with her. But I like imagining a scene where she would be angry and silent and then I would say the perfect line and she would smile and hug me. It never happened though. Shit.

"No, I told you, I was always the one to leave them."

She looks back at her monitor; now she can't help but talk. I know. I wait for her. I turn on my computer and pretend to wait for the screen to light up.

"My parents got divorced when I was ten," she says suddenly. "My father left us with my mother and grandmother. He did the right thing by leaving: my mother was crazy. She committed suicide five years ago."

I look at her. The light from the screen reflects in her green eyes. I think I see something clouding them over. I move to get up and hug her but she puts out an arm and stops me, without even turning towards me.

"No," she says. "There's no need. It's past. I've got over it and I'm better."

I'm caught half standing, knees bent and arse raised off the chair. Undecided whether to get up or sit down, I decide to stand at the very moment the boss enters the room. He looks at me strangely, having seen me get up suddenly and with no apparent reason. He looks at me as if I've done something wrong.

"Do either of you know where there is a three-way socket with a German adaptor?" he asks. Luisa doesn't move. The boss looks at me. "We spend a tonne of money on extension leads and various things, but when you look for them they're never there. Now why is that?"

"Who knows?" I say, raising my hands in the air.

The doorbell rings. The boss stays where he is until he remembers that he is his own secretary today and he runs as if he's been bitten by a tarantula.

"Shit!" he says, leaving the room. "Alex, find the extension lead for me! And with a German adaptor plug!"

Where on earth will I find it? He's right, though. We buy a lot of stuff and when you need something it's never there. I look around, staring at the boxes and the cupboards with overwhelming fatigue. I can't even get up the strength to open them. Numbers 1–9 all at once; the job seems impossible.

"There's one under here," Luisa says. "I don't need it. It's yours if you can get it."

She points under her desk and as soon as I bend down I see what she means. Luisa's desk is low and it's closed in the front and the sides by a plastic panel that makes it seem like a rectangular box, filled with dustballs, jumbled wires and plugs. The extension lead is all the way at the back in the far corner. I have to bend down and slide underneath the desk to get it.

"Shit," I mumble, breathing in dust and heat from the hard drive. Luisa giggles, and moves her legs, but not very much, only the bare minimum for me to get by. I wriggle in further, pulling myself along on one elbow, sliding on my side. I see the lead, but then I also see something else. Luisa'a silver anklet. The chain is thin and hangs loosely around her tanned ankle. There's a heart charm on the chain. I don't know why, but I reach out and touch it with the tip of my finger.

Luisa moves her leg. She slips off her sandal and gently places her foot on my head, pushing me down slightly. I can't tell if it is a gesture to push me away, or a rough friendly caress, the way you'd pat a dog, or something else. I don't know, but all of a sudden I feel a strange blade of desire jab me like a knife in the stomach, causing me to suddenly get a hard on. At that very moment, from behind the plastic wall that covers me, I hear a voice enter the room.

"You must be Luisa."

It's not the boss's voice, or Mauri's. It's a voice I don't know. Who is it?

I hear something like a cough. Luisa's foot slides down my shoulder and is suddenly very heavy.

I'm scared.

Luisa's arm flops down on her lap, hits her thigh and then hangs there, the cigarette still between her semi-clenched fingers.

I'm scared.

The man who spoke is still in the room. He hasn't moved. I hear him move behind the plastic box that covers me. He doesn't say anything, he doesn't do anything, he might not even be breathing, but I hear him.

I'm scared.

I have no thoughts, no feelings, no reaction. I am an empty tube covered with frozen, exposed nerves. It seems like everything around me is dilating. Me, too. I am out of focus and blurry; I have no breath. No thoughts, no rational activity, no ideas. I feel like ice on a terminal of nerves, a single frozen breath. How long do I remain like that?

I hear the man move, I hear his steps, the grinding of dust under his shoes. He goes out of the room.

I suddenly come to my senses. The ice on my nerves melts into an intense prickle. Cold sweat soaks my hair at the collar of my shirt. My elbow aches from leaning on it on the floor. The side of my body is senseless. I start to wonder, what the hell happened? Who was that? What was that? Luisa . . .

I slide out from underneath the table, trying not to make any noise. I grab on to the side of the desk but when I pull on it the plastic makes a cracking noise. I don't know if it's strong enough. But when I see Luisa, when I see her head tipped back and the black holes where her eyes used to be, I scream, and I know that the scream is mine.

I hear a noise in the boss's office. Rubber soles moving across the terracotta tiles, making them shake. As soon as I saw Luisa, I had jumped back towards the door. Now, I throw myself against it and close it before he comes. It slams in his face and I push on it with my shoulder. I see him whip his head back, his face contorted in a grimace of pain. He pulls his fingers out of the door just before I squash them.

There's no key. I lean against the door, dig my feet into the floor and hold steady. He pushes against it, but he's no stronger than I am and when I lean a heel against Luisa's desk and the desk doesn't move, I realise he won't be able to get in.

He knows it too, because he stops pushing.

"Alessandro . . ." he says, from behind the door. "Open up, please."

Damned if I will. I push harder. I thank God that Freeskynet is located in an old palazzo in the historic centre of town, with old-fashioned doors and locks. I swear to myself that if I get out of this alive I will find the money to restore the frescoes on the ceiling. In that moment I think a lot of stupid things, and if I weren't me, I'd be surprised at how many stupid things you can think of all at once, and so quickly too, at certain moments.

Something presses against the door, something that doesn't go through the wood. Two small explosions, as if someone had tried hammering in a nail that was too short. Only two.

"Alessandro, please."

I stay where I am. Something has to happen. Someone has to arrive. I stay where I am. The only entrance to this room is through the door I'm holding and if I stay still, without moving a millimetre, he can't come in. There's a window at my shoulder, but we're on the second floor. He can't fly. He's still there, by the door, in the boss's office. I hear him move around. He tears some paper. He moves some furniture. He unzips something.

I hear a splash, the heavy thud of something dense hitting the floor. Liquid dripping against the wall and the floor. Against the door.

I jump back when I see a pink liquid wash under the door and halfway into the room. I yell when the bitter smell of petrol forces me to close my throat. I close my eyes, but the fire is visible, even through the skin of my closed eyelids.

A second later the door opens.

Without thinking, because if I thought about it I wouldn't have done it, I turn and run and jump out the window.

Thank God for the porticoes in Bologna. I fall onto one of the roofs and roll down the tiles without stopping. I bang my arms and legs and when I manage to regain control of them it's too late: I fly over the edge and fall to the ground.

I land on the street, like a sack. Flat on my back. The fall knocks the wind out of me and tangles up my kidneys with a deafening pain that swells up inside me as though I were about to explode. Someone picks me up under my arms and my breath comes back to me. But it comes out in a nasty, raucous burp, like a roar.

Voices around my head.

Pain in my kidneys.

"Oh my god, are you hurt?"

"You fell from up there: what happened?"

"Call someone . . . call an ambulance . . . let him sit down."

Looking up and seeing where I fell from makes me realise that I couldn't be too injured. The columns of the porticoes are only a little taller than I am. I must have covered a lot of distance by rolling down the roof. I pull away from the man who is holding me up and try to take a step.

"I'm fine," I say. I'm confused. I can't think straight. I'm still blocking out the thought of Luisa.

Then I see him.

I know it's him from the way he looks at me. He's standing under the porticoes. He has a hand tucked into the pocket of his leather waistcoat and a cut on his forehead which is bleeding. His hair is died red and he has a ring in his left nostril. He looks young at first sight, but he doesn't seem so young. He has an undefinable age. He looks at me; it looks as if he's waiting for me, but I can't think straight. I'm scared. Not like before, but I'm still scared. I don't know what to do, how to get away from there.

The man that was holding me up puts out his hand to steady me because I'm shaking all over.

"Where are you going? Stay here, you're hurt."

"Leave him alone. Look at him, he's a drug addict."

"He fell from up there. Look, there's a fire."

When everyone turns to look up I take advantage of the distraction and move away. One step after another under the porticoes, my arms wrapped around me, grasping my sides.

He follows me.

Matera, at the door.
"Grazia? A call just came in. Hurry."

I HAVE TO WALK SLOWLY. MY ELBOW ACHES AND I'M limping, but I keep walking. I know I look truly insane: dusty, grimy, one hand caked with blood, clothes torn on one elbow and knee. I look like a junkie in a state of delirium. People move aside when I pass by but I simply walk towards a place where there are more people. When the portico empties I cross over and go to the other side. And I keep walking, slowly.

He follows me. But always a few metres back. He keeps his hand in his pocket. He doesn't pull it out and doesn't get any closer. At least not for now, while there are people around.

I could grab someone and begin to yell: "It's him! It's him!" but I'm afraid that the people would run away and leave me alone under the porticoes. Besides, I don't even know who he actually is. Maybe if I saw a policeman . . . but there are none around right now.

He follows me down the road. When I pick up the pace he walks faster and when I stop to cross the road, he doesn't even pretend to look into a window, he just stops and watches me. He doesn't get close to me because he's probably afraid that I'll grab someone and begin to scream. He has other plans for me. He wants to kill me, but not here.

The distance from work to my house never seemed so long. I don't live far away. My apartment is on a road that intersects with via Zamboni, at the end of a road that crosses Piazza Maggiore and passes in front of Feltrinelli's: all places that are filled with people, even at this early hour. Women coming out of shops. Students. Taxi drivers waiting in Piazza Maggiore. Students. Immigrants selling their wares on the ground under the porticoes of via Ugo Bassi. Students, students and more students. Bologna never seemed so crowded. A group of people is trying to cross the street between the two towers, being careful not to get hit by a bus. I cross in the middle of them. And him? He stops a few metres away and looks at me. And then he follows me.

Maybe if I was a little more lucid, if I hadn't just jumped out of the second storey window of a burning building, if I hadn't been under a desk when a guy killed my best friend, maybe I could do something. Escape, call for help, shield myself with a child, something. But nothing comes to mind. So I keep walking. I can't just hide in the entranceway to a building. If it's closed or deserted, this guy will come and shoot me. I can't run down a side street because I can't run; he would catch me and kill me. I can't hail a taxi because, first of all, one wouldn't stop for a person in my condition, but even if one did, the man would climb right in and kill both me and the taxi driver. It's like a videogame. I have to keep going; I've used up all the lives I had and now I just have to keep going. If the adversary catches up with me I'll flicker and then the screen will go dark. Game over.

I cross via Ravegnana and pass in front of Feltrinelli's. For a moment I think about slipping in there, going through the turnstile at the entrance but instead I push ahead. If I go in, I shorten the distance between us; he'll catch up with me and kill me. So I keep going. I walk around a huddle of bicycles piled up against a wall. I head down via Zamboni.

He follows me. His hand is in his pocket and his eyes are fixed on me. The cut on his forehead has stopped bleeding and a dried, crusted line of blood trails almost to his eyebrow.

My apartment isn't far away. It's at the end of this road, on the left, down a long, deserted, narrow alleyway. At the corner of my street there's a bar, an Irish pub; it's closed now, but there are tables outside and there are always people sitting at them, talking, passing the time. I stop for a second, still shaky on my feet, my arms wrapped around me. At first everyone looks at me. Then they ignore me and just peer up at me from time to time; nervous, suspicious.

He waits. He seems to know what I want to do. A group of people passes and turns down the alley. I follow them to my building. He closes in, anticipating my move.

When I am just a metre away from home, I start to run. My whole body aches: my head, my back, my kidneys, my legs, my elbow, but I try to run anyway. I lean forward and push off with the tips of my toes, my elbows pumping at the air. If it was any further away I wouldn't be able to do it, but the entranceway and the two steps that lead in are right there. I throw myself inside. I grab on to the door and slam it behind me with all the strength that I have, because if I manage to shut the door in his face, I'm safe, but the door is attached to the wall by a chain, damn, and it doesn't close all the way. My hand loses hold of it, pain runs through my arm as though all my fingers have broken. I fly up the stairs, three at a time, grabbing the railing. I'm sure I won't make it because I live on the third floor and there's no-one around and also because he runs faster than I do and soon he'll catch up with me and kill me.

Signora Righi's pram is leaning up against the door on the first floor landing. I grab it and throw it behind me. For now, that pram saves my life.

I get to my floor. I'm alone. I dig into my pocket for the keys. I'm sure that I have too little advantage over him, I know he's going to come up behind me and kill me. But instead I manage to open the door and run inside.

Dog pushes at me and makes me fall flat on the floor. A second passes before I gather myself together and then turn to see the empty doorway. I kick the door closed.

"Morbido!" I shout, but he doesn't answer. I push Dog away: he's licking my face. I try to get up, but my whole body hurts and I fall back down on my knees.

"Shit!" I yell at Dog. He moves away and looks at me, his head on one side, puzzled. I lean on the wall and pull myself up, reaching for the telephone. When I pick up the receiver, I stupidly think that I don't need to write down the 113 emergency number in the notebook because it's a free call. But I don't even dial it. There's no dial tone. Just silence.

Dog looks up at the door.

He lifts his face and looks at the entrance; he takes a step and then stops. He lowers his head, curls back his lips in a snarl, reveals his teeth and begins to growl.

I see the door shaking. The handle vibrates, as if someone on the other side were trying to open it. The chain is dangling uselessly on the side of the door. I look at the crack between the door and the frame and notice that I didn't even turn the lock once. It's only the closed door, no bolt. I don't have the courage to move. I should jump up, turn the lock and put the chain on, but I can't. As soon as I think about it, he calls me from outside.

"Alessandro. Please."

Dog is growling. He sounds like a diesel engine: an uninterrupted low rumble. The sound varies only when he has to catch his breath. And even then he doesn't seem to interrupt the sound; he just starts once more. When the door starts rattling again Dog barks once, his jaws snapping rapidly. It's like an explosion: so dry it doesn't even seem to echo in the corridor. The door stops shaking. The man stays there for a minute, an immobile silhouette. Then, suddenly, on the landing, something snaps, something metallic, a sound that reminds me of movies with guns. A second later, I hear a scraping. A thin piece of metal sticks out between the lock and begins to move back and forth, from right to left.

Dog barks. He fills the corridor with his noise; it piles up on top of itself, it chokes itself. He gets close to the door, but he doesn't touch it. He takes a step back, gingerly, and begins barking again. I can't take it any more. I throw myself against the wall, slide down to the ground and move into a corner. I cover my ears with my arms and begin to scream, but I can't hear it because the sound gets lost in the wild, ferocious howling of Dog. The only other noise I can hear is the grinding of the metal in the lock. Something has already begun to move: half a turn to the right and half a turn to the left. He's going to come in now and kill me.

Suddenly Dog stops barking. He stops growling, too. The sudden silence fills my ears. It whispers inside my head, my eardrums feel as though they are going to explode from the inside.

"Bark!" I yell. "Don't stop. Bark! Growl, damn it! Bark!"

Terror makes my blood run cold. I shiver. He whispers quietly, but now it's not just one voice, it's many. "Alessandro, open the door." I press my hands up against my ears and yell. The door is slowly opening. I shut my eyes and scream; I lay on the floor curled up like a frightened child and scream; my mouth is wide open on the cold tiles. I scream because something touches me. I feel hands on my head, lifting me up and pressing me against a shoulder. It feels like a woman, it feels like a mother. She holds me, I feel warm fabric and skin and hear a woman's voice: "It's all right, it's over, calm down now. I'm with the police, Ispettore Negro. Calm down now, calm down."

I look at the woman who's holding me in her arms, on her knees next to me. An older man is standing in the doorway with a gun in his hands, which he points towards the ceiling. He looks at Dog with a frightened look in his eye.

"Watch out, Negro, that's a pit bull!"

I take a deep breath to summon all the voice I have left and speak through the tears that burn my throat.

"No," I say, "it's a Staffordshire bull terrier . . . looks like a pit bull . . . but it's not."

THOUGHT: IT'S NOT HARD TO LOOK LIKE ANOTHER person.

First of all, there's the hair: hair does a lot. The longer your hair, the more your face changes. It covers your face and creates shadows that make it seem thinner. When you have no hair you look older. Bristly, thick hair makes you look tough. You can wear hair in a pony tail or die it or shave it or wear it parted on the side. Hair is easy to work with. All you have to do is keep your own hair very short, squash it down with a net and put on a wig with a good fixative. A Glatzan skullcap can even change the shape of your head.

Next come the eyes: you can get contact lenses in almost every colour, but there's more to it than that. You can depilate and shape your eyebrows. You can thicken them with extra hair; you can distance them or unite them. Eyebrows change the shape of your eyes, even your whole face.

Teeth: fundamental. Healthy white, dazzling fake white, or unhealthy yellow ones. A good prosthesis, even a half one, can puff up the lips or make them look thinner, changing the entire shape of the face. Beard and sideburns: obvious. Cushions and padding: widen the shoulders, stomach, hips and backside. These are banalities.

Nose: grease makes a good base when you use prostheses made of latex and plaster. Skin: Kryolan Dermacolor foundation comes in tubes of 15 grams each. Wrinkles at the corners of the eyes, age spots on the backs of hands. Nicotine stains on fingers. Cuts, calluses, broken nails.

Movements. Posture. Nervous tics. Every person has their own speed. The rhythm of gestures: slow, rigid, restrained, fast, frenetic, soft, smooth.

There must always be some kind of detail. Avoid the typical. A contradiction always makes things more authentic. When something is noticeable everything else blends into the background and stays out of focus. A man who limps is The Man Who Limps. A boy with a piercing is The Boy with a Piercing. An old man with prostate problems and a broken nose is The Old Man with Prostate Problems and a Broken Nose. Careful not to let the detail become so strong that it triggers people's interest and causes them to observe the rest more carefully, too. The detail has to reveal itself gradually, when you think about it; it has to impose itself over everything else and catalyse the memory. Yes, I think he limped, but which leg was it? The left one, I think. Yes, it was the left, now I remember. I can see it now. He was The Man that Limped. Always think of who your witnesses will be. Adapt. Adapt. Adapt.

Thought: it's not hard to look like another person. It's hard to be another person.

With his car parked at the roadside restaurant, hidden from view behind two parked trucks, Vittorio looked into the rear-view mirror to make sure the dark tinted foundation was spread evenly over his face. He completed his preparations by spreading the foundation on his neck, under his shirt line, spreading some on his hands, too, rubbing them together. He had already plugged the hair-straightening iron into the cigarette lighter and its long metal beak was hot. He took a handful of short salt-and-pepper hair from a bag on the passenger seat, flattened it with the iron and then shaped it to his face under his nose and around his chin in a small, well-maintained, grey goatee. He did the same with sideburns, which he kept short, and then he chose a wig from the bag that was of the same colour, with short hair, slightly balding. Raising himself up to look into the mirror he checked to make sure that the latex skullcap fit perfectly and that it blended seamlessly in with his skin. He took a pair of thin tweezers and scraped away bits of foundation at the corners of his eyes and his mouth. From a small case inside his bag, he withdrew a small prosthesis that covered his four front teeth, making them larger and whiter than normal.

At that point he leaned back and looked at himself in the mirror from a distance: a good-looking man, between 40 and 50, tanned, with those thin, light wrinkles that people who spend time at the seaside have. A good-looking man who cares about his appearance. Maybe closer to 50 than 40 . . . see? he has false teeth.

Vittorio nodded, content. He hoped it was still hot in Sabaudia. From the boot of the car, in keeping with his persona, he took out a black, short-sleeved polo shirt.

ALEX FAINTED AT CASUALTY BUT NOT BECAUSE OF HIS wounds. The smell of alcohol and medicine that was always present in those places made him faint, the white neon light and the false, heavy silence that was charged with tension made him faint. He always fainted at casualty, once even when he went to accompany a friend. He told Grazia about it. She pretended to listen. He was laid out on the trolley, naked from the waist up, one arm stretched out to the side so that the doctor could clean the abrasion on his elbow. Grazia had so many questions for him. She was on edge because she thought he might faint again, so she let him talk a little and nodded maternally. Commissario Carlisi was there, too, sitting in the armchair. Matera was leaning against the door.

"You were really lucky, kid," Matera said.

"I know," Alex said, being careful not to move because they hadn't put his neck brace on yet; it was next to him on the trolley. "I was barely hurt at all."

"No, I mean you were lucky that we . . ."

He stopped when Grazia cast him a fast and hard look. He had been on the point of explaining how they found him. The fire had stopped at the door to the room where he worked, without touching Luisa's body. The first people there called the police. The police laboratory wasn't far away, just across the piazza, and when one of their colleagues found the plastic and glass bullet he immediately called the Mobile Unit, who had been pestering everyone for days for information about that particular type of bullet. Of the three employees at the office who were missing they had decided to look for Alex first because his apartment was the closest. It turns out that the other two, Mauri and the secretary, had been killed the night before.

Matera wasn't supposed to mention any of this. Alex was already in a state of shock, he was as light as a feather and numbed by the tranquilliser that flowed through his veins. Free from thought. Eventually he would begin to remember what happened, but right now Grazia just wanted him to talk. After he heard Matera, however, he fell silent. He went pale; the doctor slapped him a few times across the cheek.

"Stay with us, kid . . . come on . . . there we go."

Alex's lips began to tremble. Grazia turned back to look at Matera, who had got up to leave the room. Then she took Alex by the shoulders and felt his forehead.

"Wait," she said. "Wait."

"Luisa," mumbled Alex, "Luisa."

"Wait, Alex, hold on a second, please."

The commissioner got up and patted the doctor on the shoulder, who in turn nodded. He took a syringe from the table and slipped the needle into the rubber top of a phial. Grazia turned Alex's face towards her, she pressed down on his mouth, as if to make him be quiet, to stop his lips from trembling.

"Wait, Alex. I'll tell you. Luisa is dead. They killed her. They wanted to kill you too, but we got there in time and now you're safe. It's over now, for you anyway. But for us it's just beginning. You have to tell us everything you know . . ."

Alex closed his eyes, squeezing away two large tears, which began to roll down his cheeks. He sucked in his saliva with a deep intake of breath, the way children do, and he shook his head. Grazia tried to keep him still and bent over him, hugging him. She felt him contract stiffly for a moment when the doctor stuck the needle in his arm, and then he collapsed, almost immediately.

"I want to get out of here," he whispered to her through her hair, "I want to leave this place."

"You will, stay calm. You'll go wherever you want. Where do you want to go? Home? We'll take you there."

"I want to go to Kristine . . . to Copenhagen, to see Kristine." He tried to sit up but Grazia stopped him. She let go of his head and stood up, but continued to hold him still, one hand on his chest. Alex looked into her eyes.

"I want Kristine," he said. "She's the only thing I want. Can't I have at least one thing from this shitty life? I want to go to her . . ."

"You'll go, it's not a problem. We'll get you a ticket, we'll pay for it and we'll put you on the plane."

"I have a dog."

"We'll put him on the plane too. Don't worry. They take dogs on planes. But you've got to answer a few questions for me, though. It was a man, right? One man, on his own?"

"Yes, a guy with a piercing."

"Don't worry about the physical description. It doesn't matter. Tell us why he did it. Why he wanted to kill you. Why he killed Luisa."

Alex sighed and closed his eyes. Grazia looked at the doctor, anxious, but he shook his head, no. No, he hadn't fallen asleep. Alex sighed again and opened his eyes.

"I don't know," he said.

"A motive. There must have been a motive. Think about it for a second. Please."

"I don't know."

"Something strange must have happened to you . . . something you did, something someone told you."

"I don't know."

She was so frustrated she wanted to punch him, tighten her hand into a fist and knock some straight answers out of him, but instead she tightened one hand inside the other, biting her lip. She felt so exasperated. The commissioner took her arm and led her away from the bed.

"Don't worry, he'll come around again. He'll get better, and then we can interrogate him calmly. Something will come out of it, you'll see."

"Yes, but when? He was on the verge of talking, Commissario. He was so close. We need him now, not tomorrow."

Outside Alex's room Matera's phone began to ring. It was supposed to be the sound of a salsa, but the electronic notes were so monotonous and acute that it could have been anything.

"Sarrina? What's that? Say it again, I can't hear a damn thing. No, wait, let me go outside, the reception in here is bad." He stuck his head back into the room. "It's Sarrina, he's calling from the Questura. He said that the old brigadiere that we were looking for is there, but I don't know who he means. I'm going outside for a minute."

"I'm coming too," Grazia said. She went back to the bed because she had left her jacket hanging on the doctor's chair. He, in the mean time, was standing and talking to the commissioner. Under observation. Keep an eye on him. Better here or somewhere else?

Grazia looked at the half-naked, scraped-up boy lying there on the trolley with his eyes closed. Lying down like that he looked even thinner, his stomach dipped into his torso as a concave hollow, rising and falling with each breath. He wasn't bad, she thought, not bad at all.

Alex opened his eyes slightly and looked at her foggily. He opened his mouth and moved his lips, as if he was looking for his voice somewhere, but found it too late, out of sync with his mouth.

"Do you think . . . I should go see Kristine?"

Grazia thought about all the druggies that she had met when she was on the beat. Sometimes they would say things to her, some kind of bullshit, and she would just nod silently. But this time she gave a straight answer.

"Yes," she said. "You should go. Whatever it is, it's always better to talk about it. Even if it doesn't work out, at least you will have tried. But listen, there's something I have to tell you. The Commissario's Office can't pay for your trip to Copenhagen after all."

Alex smiled. He shut his eyes and sniffled, but sleepily, as if it were difficult. He couldn't keep his eyes open any more. Grazia slipped her jacket off the doctor's chair. She was about to leave when she felt Alex's hand grab her wrist.

"Listen, I don't remember your name – Ispettore Negro, was it? Listen, maybe something strange did happen to Luisa and me."

Matera was standing near the window to get better reception and had just shut his mobile phone when Grazia and the commissioner walked out of the hospital room.

"The brigadiere from the Carabinieri command in Como is here," he said. "He wants to talk to us."

"Forget about the brigadiere," Grazia said. "Call Sarrina and tell him to get over here. We may have found our link to Pit Bull."

She walked off briskly down the corridor, while the commissioner ran up to the window where Matera had been standing and leaned out to dial 113 on his phone. He was calling to warn the commissioner in Sabaudia to send someone to Avvocato D'Orrico's house quickly. Very quickly.

"What was that noise? Sovrintendente, did you hear that noise? It sounded like someone was lowering the blinds."

"Go get Pistocchi. Where's Pistocchi?"

"He went back over that way. There was a man walking along the beach; he went to tell him to pick up shells somewhere else. Hey, Sovrintendente, did you hear that? It's that noise again . . ."

"JUST ONE PATROL CAR? EXCUSE ME, YOU SENT ONLY one patrol car for three men?"

Twisting around in the front seat, Grazia tried to look beyond the headrest at the Vice Questore Bruzzini. He had made her sit in the front seat, or rather, he had slipped into the back of the blue Alfa and didn't move over, leaving her standing there with the door handle in her hand, implying that she would have to sit in the front seat with the driver, while Matera and Sarrina followed in their own car. He looked at her in surprise, a little amazed, as if it were the first time someone had criticised him.

"Excuse me, what do you mean?" he said. "What should I have sent?"

"But, don't you get it? Didn't Dottore Carlisi tell you?"

"Dottore Carlisi is a commissario from the Bologna Mobile Unit. I am the Vice Questore here and this is my territory. What is your rank, signorina?"

"Ispettore Capo," Grazia replied. Her back was beginning to hurt in that position and she would have liked to sit normally, but at that point it would have seemed rude to turn around. Instead she wrapped her other hand around the headrest and grabbed it as if she wanted to strangle it.

"Call them, please," she said. "Call your men at the villa and tell them to be careful."

Bruzzini put his hand in his jacket and reached for the

telephone that was hooked to his belt. He flipped up the antenna and then stopped. There was something about that girl's manner that worried him, even if she was only chief inspector. She didn't even have a university degree. She was one of those girls who thinks she's a kind of Rambo and who probably likes to wear her gun while she fucks. Bruzzini looked at Grazia's arm, her small dark hand, her wrist, her fingers and their short, rounded nails. How old is she? he wondered to himself. Probably 26 or so. He felt the need to adjust his balls because even though she wasn't his type – she wasn't stunning and was sort of swarthy – underneath her clothes she must be smooth and toned like . . . like a girl. But there was something serious in her gaze, something competent and responsible that caught his attention. He held on to his mobile phone and placed his other hand on his knee, smoothing down the lightweight fabric of his trousers.

"Marenco," he said to the driver. "Call the Sovrintendente and see how things are going."

Grazia loosened her grip and sat back down in the chair, as Marenco unhooked the microphone from the CB radio and asked the operator at headquarters to call the sovrintendente on his mobile.

"What can I do?" Bruzzini was saying. "I don't have an army or anything. There's the division of the National Alliance here in Sabuadia, but they're just a network of sluts of various shape and colour who come from Latina. You have no idea how hard it is to work with them. Anyway, I had only one car available. Besides, who is so pissed off with Avvocato D'Orrico?"

"Dottore, the sovrintendente isn't answering."

Grazia squeezed her armrest so tightly her knuckles turned white.

"He must have turned it off," Bruzzini said.

"No, Dottore, it just keeps ringing."

Grazia turned around and knelt on her seat to face him, the way children do, grabbing the headrest with her hands.

"Dottore . . ." she said.

"He must have left it lying around somewhere," Bruzzini said. "He must have left it in the car. Get the number and call the villa. They must be inside."

"Dottore, let's go a little faster, please."

Bruzzini sat up and straightened his jacket. He was getting nervous. There was something about this girl. Something that flustered him.

"What's the rush?" he said. "I sent three men, three strong men, not children. Sovrintendente Barra, special agent Pistocchi and Carlini (agent, or assistant, I can't remember which). All policemen. What on earth could happen to them?"

Grazia shook her head. She pulled out her mobile from her jacket and flipped it open. She pressed the call button twice to access the last number dialled, which was Sarrina's.

"Sarri', put your siren on and get over to the villa. Go straight along this road . . ."

She closed her phone by slapping it against her backside and watched through the rear window as Matera clamped the magnetic base of the blue light to the roof of the car. Bruzzi looked first at Grazia, then at the car that overtook them and then swerved back into the lane in front of them, speeding off and trailing the sound of the siren.

"How dare you . . ." he stammered. "How dare you? Who the hell are you?"

"Dottore, no-one's answering the phone at the villa, either."

"Why?" he said, wondering out loud. "Where are they? Have they left? What did they do? My men . . ."

"Stop, Dottore," Grazia said, bending down to look for the siren under her seat. "Your men are dead."

The villa was close to the beach and linked to the road by a wooden bridge that crossed over a dune of dirty sand mixed with patches of dry, yellow grass. On the road, one wheel in the sand, was Matera and Sarrina's car, the light from the siren still flashing. The two of them had just arrived and were standing on the edge of the crossing, their guns in hand. Marenco stopped the Alfa a little further ahead, close to the ramp in the main road. Grazia jumped out and ran to them. She pulled out her gun and pointed it down at the ground.

"Look," Bruzzini said, pointing to the blue-and-white car that was parked behind the villa, near two paths of trampled sand. "They're here, you see?"

Grazia didn't even look at him. She released the barrel of her Beretta and began to walk towards the path, her arm raised, gun in the air, ready to shoot. Sarrina kept her in sight and held his gun with both his hands, aiming at the villa. Matera cut across the dune with his gun raised, too.

The villa was a white, square building. It looked small from the road, not much bigger than a cabin with no doors or windows facing the main road. But all you needed to do was look at it from the side to see that it wasn't so. It stretched all the way down to the sea, and was built on a foundation of wood to even it out with the dune. It wasn't attractive; from the side it looked like a big warehouse. The walkway ran parallel along it, almost down to the water, following a row of closed windows that worried Grazia. The entrance must be on the other side, facing the sea.

The sun was going down. The light was metallic; even the air that came from the ocean, salty and smelling of rotten seaweed, had a ferrous quality to it. Matera ran down the dune until he reached the end of the house and peered cautiously in through the first window. Having glanced in, he retreated. Sarrina stopped on the pathway, his gun raised. Grazia kept going.

"Pistocchi! Sovrintendente Barra!"

Grazia dropped to the ground so quickly that her bottom hit the back of her heels. If her finger had been on the trigger instead of the bridge, a shot would have gone off. She saw Sarrina making an angry gesture at Bruzzini, who stopped shouting and stood frozen at the beginning of the path. Then she turned back towards the villa. From where she was sitting she saw something behind the dunes, further ahead. She got up and ran almost to the end of the pathway, where she stood on her tiptoes and saw with clarity what she had feared. It was Special Agent Pistocchi, lying on his back, arms over his face, his legs spread wide and his torso torn open by gunfire all the way to his lungs. From the boot prints in the sand and the position of his beret, the shot must have thrown him at least two metres.

"Shit," murmured Grazia. She beckoned to Sarrina to come closer and then ran towards the door of the villa, which was ajar. She waited there for Sarrina and Matera, who leaned against the wall, breathing heavily.

"There's one guy in the living room. I think he's dead."

He was. Grazia saw him as soon as she pushed open the door. Sovrintendente Barra. He had fallen face first over a chair, his arms were behind his back and his head had fallen forwards, it was practically touching the floor. On the smooth terracotta, shining in the dusky light of the sunset, were the marks of the gunfire that had ripped open his arm to the bone.

It was getting dark, but the white linen sheets which covered the sofas and armchairs in the living room reflected the last rays of sunshine, creating a strange play of shadows.

"Should we turn on the light?" Sarrina asked.

"Better not," Matera said.

Grazia moved quickly out of the doorway and went into the living room. The others followed; Matera, who had seen through the window, proceeded down the corridor. There were three rooms on the left, all of them empty, as he had seen from outside.

There was one more room on the right-hand side. Matera hadn't looked in there yet.

All three of them walked down the dark hallway towards it. Grazia thought about the shells she saw on the floor next to Barra's body. A machine gun. If Pit Bull came out of that room he would get all three of them in the hallway with one round. Then something fell down next to her with a sticky thud. Grazia froze, as if in a child's game: caught you! come out!

"Shit!" Sarrina yelled, and then even more hysterically: "Holy Shit! I fell on a corpse! One of our guys! I'm covered with blood! Fuck! Fuck! Fuck!"

"Carlini," Grazia said. "Only D'Orrico is left. Christ. He got them all."

"At least he didn't kill them right under our noses," mumbled Matera. "Let's go into the last room."

He and Grazia entered the room together. Sarrina couldn't get to his feet, he kept slipping. As soon as they walked in they saw him: his profile blended in with what seemed like an armchair, a black outline against the bloody red light of sunset that shone through the window. They lowered their guns with a sigh and Matera turned on the light.

Avvocato D'Orrico opened his eyes.

"I've been waiting for you," he said.

D'ORRICO'S VOICE SEEMED CALM. HE SPOKE IN LONG monologues which he allowed to be interrupted only to answer specific questions. His tape recorded voice came out sounding direct, confident, even relieved at times. There was an irony and false modesty in his voice, he accentuated the final syllables of his words. He sounded calm.

But Grazia could tell that he wasn't. She had spent too many hours with earphones on, listening to intercepted phone calls time and again; both recorded and live, cleaned of noise or fuzzy with interference; in Italian; in dialect and even in foreign languages. She could recognise the details.

For one thing, D'Orrico was smoking. She couldn't see him – she wasn't present when the magistrate interrogated him – but she could tell from listening to him. He interrupted his sentences with a very brief suspended silence of less than a second and when he'd begin again his voice would come out as being more veiled over than before, smoky. A puff of a cigarette. She could hear when he exhaled. Expert smokers, those who have been smoking for a long time, show they are as much in the way they construct their sentences: they order their words around taking the next puff, they don't just do it in the middle of a sentence. Cigar smokers are recognisable by their inhalations, which are less frequent and separated by a wider space, because you smoke cigars more slowly than you do cigarettes, and because a lot of cigar smokers, especially those who smoke Toscanos, keep them in their mouth when they talk, clenched between their teeth, with their voice coming out in a kind of unpunctuated drawl. That was how Grazia had been able to recognise a Slav in the Bolognina: he was one of only two suspects that smoked a cigar.

But D'Orrico didn't smoke in any of those ways; he smoked a lot. He smoked too much. He took one puff after another in the quick pauses that gradually became more difficult to recognise. They started to seem like a deliberate cadence, typical of the way a lawyer speaks. He spoke smoothly but wasn't calm. He seemed sure of himself because he talked a lot, but his sentences didn't always go anywhere. His words, at times, seemed chosen only to fill a space, to fill a silence that must have scared him. D'Orrico wasn't calm, he was shitting himself. His whole effort went into camouflaging the fear in his voice.

"I met Pit Bull in August, 1996," he said. "It was he who first made contact with me – but not in person. He found me through a website for those with a particular kind of sexual preference that I don't want to talk about right now (puff), even though I might choose to do so later on, if and when my crime is contested. Anyway, (puff) I don't know how he managed to get my password and address, he didn't seem interested in the website, but in other things (puff): in my knowledge, my business and finance contacts, not to mention my ties (puff) to more illegal affairs . . .

"I was a kind of agent for him, a procurator (puff); I found him clients, I gathered information on the victims and I sent it to him by e-mail, in code, to a clean address (puff). If we had to discuss something in a hurry we'd arrange, always by e-mail, to meet in a pre-determined chat room; we'd speak in private but from a public place. I always did it that way (puff) except once, and just that one time the phone rang and a girl shouted, 'We know what you're up to, you bastard!' All I had to do was look at the phone number on the display to understand that it was someone from a provider, but by then (puff) the damage was done. And to think that I never made a mistake, I never stole so much as a single lira – that's another thing: I also arranged for him to receive his payments."

Grazia looked up at her message board. On the white writing surface she had drawn a long line that connected the photo of the pit bull to another pile of Post-it notes. She had taken the number seven, "How does he get paid?" from up above and placed it at the bottom. Around it she had started to stick other Post-its with names of banks and current-account numbers, but then she had stopped adding them; Carlisi had put two other agents from the Unit to work on it and even brought in the Finanza. In the same way she stopped adding notes to question number three, which read "Good with weapons. Where does he get them?" D'Orrico had explained that point to them in detail towards the end of the tape.

"Do you think I didn't look for him? (puff) That I didn't do everything I could to work out who and where he was? He prohibited me from doing it (longer puff, the crackle of a cigarette being lit), but I did it anyway, for two reasons. First of all: among our clients were a few people who would have been willing to pay generously to turn the contract around and have the killer killed. For me, Pit Bull was the goose that laid the golden egg, but a few times I got an offer (puff) that was very difficult to refuse. Secondly (puff): I wanted to cover my back. It didn't seem like I was the first procurator for Pit Bull, and I wondered what happened to the other men like me. How long would I last? (puff) So I looked for him but I never found him. When he contacted me he always did it by e-mail or from chat rooms on public computers. I traced the money but (puff) got mired in a series of numbered accounts that skipped from one bank to another, from Switzerland to San Marino, and then disappeared over the border. The only description I was able to get was of a certain Dottore

Franz (puff) who deposited and withdrew cash continuously, who was a man of around 70, with a scar on his nose and who, in any case, had already closed down his account six months earlier (puff). I tried to find out who he was through his weapons and the bullets, through everything he used to complete his contracts, but I couldn't. His weapons don't come from any conventional channels of the *malavita*, neither Italian nor foreign (puff). As you know, it's not difficult to buy a machine gun from the Croatians or bombs from the Albanians and if the right people ask, anyone can find out. Not with him. Either he went alone (puff) to get his reinforcements in loco and then he killed the provider (puff) or else he went to an armoury to get his weapons, but (puff) I doubt that. For the rest, he had no contacts. With anyone. It seemed as though (puff) he was more worried about being given away by some turncoat than being caught (puff) by the police."

Grazia put the tape recorder down on the pillow and got up from the camp bed on which she had been sitting. She walked over to the message board on tiptoe, because she had taken off her boots and the dirty floor bothered her. She stared at the photograph of the dog. It looked back at her ferociously, fearlessly. At first she had used the photo of a pit bull after a fight, photographed from the front while it barked crazily, its face marked with red scars, nose ripped open on one side, an ear almost torn off. She had downloaded it from the Internet and attached it to the message board, but then she had removed it and replaced it with one from a magazine. The picture of that poor dog, trained by someone to fight to the death, pained her. She didn't want to feel any pain for Pit Bull. She wanted to get him.

D'Orrico. "I, or rather, Pit Bull (puff), with my mediation, brought twelve contracts to conclusion. We called them meetings. They were always something particular: eliminations that needed a person who was *super partes*, someone who had nothing to do with the mob, someone who could eliminate a target who was under special protection or likely to be a difficult hit (puff). But even private individuals contacted me, people who simply wanted a job well done, without risks. The fact is (puff) that professional killers in Italy are still marginal figures. It used to be that it was a criminal speciality monopolised by the Mafia or done (puff) by some creep at the bar. Pit Bull was in the market to fill this niche . . ."

Grazia got so close to the photo of the pit bull that she could smell the acidy smell of the magazine paper. She got so close to it that the face of the dog slowly became a confused and opaque stain, blurry. She took one step back, then another, until the back of her legs bumped into the edge of the table. She didn't want to be confused: she wanted to see his face clearly. She had seen too many cadavers: bodies lying on floors of abandoned houses for days on end, bodies left in ditches in the countryside, photographs of corpses, bodies on mortuary tables: naked, white and obscene. She didn't want to get confused. She wanted to see his face. She wanted to put a face there, the face of a man, not of a dog. She wanted to get him.

D'Orrico. "I never saw him in person. I never spoke to him on the phone. I don't know what he looks like, his face or his body. I don't know what his name is. I was sure he was going to kill me. Instead he told me to wait here for you and tell you everything."

WHEN YOU'RE DRIVING ALONG THE MOTORWAY AND someone calls you on your mobile phone and you answer and they ask you where you are and you say, "I'm in Pescara," it's not true. You're not in Pescara: you still have two kilometres of ramps and overpasses and another nine kilometres of motorway and when you're eleven kilometres from a place you can't really say you're there. You're somewhere else. But if you stay on the phone another ten minutes and then the person says, "Sorry, where did you say you were?" you can no longer say that you are in Pescara, but in Roseto degli Abruzzi if you go north, or in Chieti if you go south. And you're not there, either, in Roseto or in Chieti, but somewhere else. You're on the motorway.

Soon the time would arrive.

Vittorio sat up and leaned forward, attempting to stretch out his vertebrae. He straightened his neck and tried to lean his head back on the headrest and arch his spine, but it didn't help. He sighed, but it was more of a hot, intense, vibrant humming sound. Not even that brought him relief. He contracted all his muscles and weary bones for a moment and then relaxed. He rested an elbow on the edge of the window, pushed up against the metal and the rubber, but after a while it began to hurt him and so he once again let his elbow drop down by his side. He moved his hands further down the wheel, from ten to two to twenty past eight.

On the motorway *being* doesn't matter. *Moving* matters. You can say you're in Pescara even when you're not because you're on your way there. For a body in continual motion, direction is more important than a precise point in space, because that point in space is no longer there. The motorway is about movement. When a car is stopped on the hard shoulder you wonder what's going on, whether the passengers are fugitives, spies or intruders. And when a car stops in one of the lanes it's even more unwelcome: it's the enemy, danger, death. The worst thing that can happen on the motorway is for a car to come to a stop: there's the squeal of brakes, a traffic jam, roads are blocked, an accident. On the motorway life is constant movement, with no inter- ruptions. That's why you stop at services only when your bladder is so full that it hurts.

Vittorio moved his legs. He leaned the side of his right shoe against the body of the car, under the dashboard, without removing his foot from the accelerator. First in one way, then in another, he tried to loosen the tendon in his ankle, which was cramped, all the time keeping the speedometer at 110 kph – white line on white line. He pulled his left knee in, rested the sole of his shoe on the rounded bump of the wheel and then shifted his position again, folding his left leg practically all the way under the right one until the side of his foot touched the carpet, but a piece of rubber stuck out and hurt his ankle bone. He felt the irresistible desire to do one of the two things that one can never do while driving: to cross your legs. The other is to close your eyes.

Thought: soon.

He had prepared everything.

He needed to find two places. One was easy, it could be anywhere, as long as it was isolated. He was sure he'd find the right place, an old hut in the Comacchio, a cabin in the Apennines, it didn't matter. The other would be more difficult, but then he found it, almost at the exit for Imola. It was off a dirt road that went down through the fields and along a narrow embankment and parallel to the foot of the flyover. A few metres further down, almost in a field, was a black tarmac road that followed a canal all the way down to the motorway. Not far off was a square metal gate, locked with a chain. Beyond the gate was the motorway.

You can do several different things while you're driving along the motorway. You can listen to music, talk on the phone, think, sing, drink, scratch yourself. You can take off your jacket with one arm, pulling it down with your hand and pushing your elbow through to make it come off, then reaching around and taking it off behind your back. You can open letters by holding the letter down on the seat next to you with the palm of your hand, then sliding a fingernail inside and tearing it, bit by bit, until you can inch your finger in like a snail. You can eat a whole container of mini salamis by sticking a knife through the plastic and cutting it open just far enough to pull them out one at a time, little round balls, held together with floury string. You can even make love, unzipping your trousers and sliding them down by pushing them back against the seat, arms taut against the wheel, teeth clenched, eyes wide open so as not to let your sight fog over. Things you can't do on the motorway: raise your legs up on the seat and assume the lotus position. Read a book or watch television. Sleep. Keep your eyes on anything other than the road.

When he noticed the service gate, Vittorio mentally registered where it was so he could try and locate it from the other side of the motorway. But it wasn't easy. On the other carriageway everything except the crash barrier, the ditch and the wire fence is completely different. The tarmac looks different, either blacker or greyer. Sometimes it's almost white. It crunches under the wheels in a different way, it scratches, it slips, it skips, or jumps. Even the crash barrier looks a little different. The countryside looks different and the service stations are different. If you don't know them well, if you happen there by chance, you might find yourself inside the narrow abode of an Alemagna, with the telephones near the newspapers and the toilets outdoors, or inside the mountain hut of a service station, with its Spizzico and its self-service restaurant, or inside the skyscraper of a Fini, with the express tortellini, or inside the bridge of a Pavesi, with the cars flashing below you. But the motorway is always the same: its geography is always linear. It doesn't follow the countryside. It cuts across it. Children draw it like a tree: with two parallel lines and single lines branching off it. It's always the same except for the exit signs. But when you get off the motorway, it's different. Right away. There's a narrow road that's like no man's land; it's no longer motorway, but it's not the real world either. You see the borders of cultivated fields, edges of factory yards, cliffs, ditches, canals, ends of gardens that belong to houses with closed windows.

That's where Vittorio had found the right place. It was a couple of kilometres from the motorway service gate. There was an old, deconsecrated church that was covered with a mass of overgrown briar; its brick walls were crumbling, one window was boarded up with wooden slats nailed across it. The roof was caving in on one side, as if a giant had sat down on it. A long time ago it must have been the chapel of a large farmhouse, but now it was nothing more than a ruin on the edge of some farmer's land. The farmer had been glad to rent it out to the man from the city who wanted to keep his camper there while he did a little fishing. They'd keep the deal under the table, of course.

Vittorio slowed down, shifted into second gear, looking for the lane that led to the toll booth. This time he'd pay in cash.

Initially he thought about driving a little van or truck, but then he decided that it wasn't a good idea because sometimes the Finanza stops vans at toll booths to check what they're carrying and that their papers are in order. A camper was better, a small camper. He stole it one night in Padova from the garage of a villa.

He brought it to the shack to paint it, put in a stereo and CB transmitter, the kind that lorry drivers have. He also attached a set of number plates to it that he had stolen from a car in the long-stay car park of an airport – the owners of the other car would probably never notice that he had switched them. Then he drove to San Marino and withdrew three hundred million lira in cash from the bank, stopped off at his office, filled a tackle chest with make-up, contact lenses, dental prostheses and wigs (all sorted by type in their own compartments), and loaded it in the camper with another chest, this one full of hooks, weights, and fishing line that covered up his .22 calibre and two silencers, which were well wrapped inside greased rags.

If his mobile had been turned on and someone, like Annalisa, had called him and asked where he was, at this point he would have said "Bologna", even though he was still far away and had the whole ring road to drive. He wanted to be home. He was tired.

MY MOTHER YELLS UP TO ME FROM DOWNSTAIRS, "Alex! It's for you!"

I lean over the balustrade and look down, but don't see her. Who knows where she is. She has this stupid habit of shouting from one room to the next without letting herself be understood. I shout back.

"Phone or door?"

"Door!"

That's strange: I didn't hear the doorbell ring. But then again, I had had my headphones on. I was in my room listening to music. I lean out a little further, almost falling. I can almost make her out: she's standing more or less in front of the door.

"Who is it?" I ask.

"I don't know! It's for you!"

"Did the police see him?"

"The police aren't here any more!"

What's she talking about: they're gone? Ever since they sent me back to my family's house in Ravenna, there's always been a patrol car in front of my house and another one that circled the block every so often. Everybody that came to the house on my first day back had to show ID to the policemen. Only on the first day, though. After that no-one else came.

I heard the front door close. My mother's voice. She's saying something like "He's upstairs, go right up." And then I hear someone coming up the stairs. I grip the banister tightly and hold my breath in fear. I hear someone climbing the first set of stairs, the sound of their fingers on the banister. Then the person turns the corner and I let out a big sigh because I see her. It's that girl from the police, the one whose name I can never remember.

"What's the matter? Did I scare you?"

"No, not at all," I say.

She follows me to my room.

"Sorry about the mess, officer."

"You don't have to be formal with me," she says.

I grab a pile of underwear and socks off the chair and throw them into the wardrobe. "They're clean," I say. "My mother just did the laundry." One sock drops on the floor; I lean down, pick it up and throw it into the wardrobe. She doesn't sit down. She walks over to the bed and picks up my headphones. The music is just barely audible.

"What are you listening to?" she asks.

I pull the plug out of the amplifier and hurry to regulate the volume, because it's too loud.

"Tenco," I reply. "'Giorno dopo l'altro'."

"Day after day," she says. "That's a sad song."

The loud explosion of music made Dog, who was asleep on the bed, raise his head. She lifts her hand to his face, keeping her distance at first, then gradually moving a little closer. He doesn't even sniff. He puts his nose down on the pillow and falls back to sleep.

"Are you sure it's not a pit bull?" she asks.

"I'm sure. He's something else."

"I brought this for you."

She passes me a folder from Alitalia. RULES AND REGULATIONS FOR THE TRANSPORTATION OF ANIMALS BY AIR. Inside there's a flyer with everything you need to know about carrying a dog overseas. I turn it over in my hands. A tight knot builds in my throat and I have to cough to dispel it.

"Thank you," I say. She looks at me and nods. She leans against the chair that I previously cleared of clothes.

"I didn't come here just to bring the folder to you," she says. "I was at the airport. I'm interrogating everybody there who had any contact with Pit Bull so I decided to stop by on my way back.'

"Pit Bull?"

"Yes, the man who wanted to kill you. That's what we call him."

"Why didn't I read about it in the papers?"

"Because we're keeping it secret. We think he has a plan in mind and we want to play his game."

"What's the plan?"

"I don't know."

"Why didn't he shoot me on the street?"

"Because he uses special bullets; it means he would have to get really close to you."

"Why does he use those bullets?"

"I don't know."

"Who is he?"

"I don't know that either."

"Will you get him?"

"Yes."

She walks around the chair and sits down. She takes off her green bomber jacket and I sneak a look at her, but not directly. I bend down and scratch Dog's ear and sneak a glance at her. She's cute. Very cute. Mediterranean. Curvy but slender. She's wearing black: a short skirt, black stockings, boots. Her bomber jacket slips off the chair and falls to the floor, the zips making a metallic sound when they land. She bends down to pick it up and a small box falls out, tumbling over my slippers. I take it off the floor and look at it.

"Oh," I say. "Are you pregnant?"

"I don't know," she says.

"Did you take the test?"

"Not yet."

She blushes, but only a little. She bites her lip and looks around, as if she is suddenly very interested in my room. "Wow, this is a sad song," she murmurs and then she tries to put the box back into her jacket pocket but can't, so she rests it on the floor near the chair. She crosses her legs. I can't help looking at her. She realises it and uncrosses her legs. She stretches them out in front of her, knees together.

"Listen, besides coming here to ask you a few questions, I also came to let you know that you don't have a post any more."

"Post?"

"The guard on duty."

I thought she meant my job at the provider. I knew I had lost that. Nothing's there any more; it burnt down; everyone's dead.

"You don't need a guard any more. We got D'Orrico and there's no reason for Pit Bull to kill you. From what I know, he has never killed anyone without a reason."

"Let's hope there's not a first time."

She smiles. She's even cuter when she smiles. She has an open smile, very real, almost infantile. When she's serious she looks a little rougher, but when she smiles you can tell she is full of life. Wild and solar. She turns her head towards the speakers, furrowing her brow.

"Is it always the same song?" she asks. And I nod because I have put Tenco on repeat, ad infinitum.

"I'm sorry, I can never remember your name."

"Ispettore Grazia Negro. Grazia."

"Like the three graces," I say, stupidly. She frowns.

"Right: Grazia, Graziella and Grazie for the fuck. Hey, watch out kid, I'm still a police officer."

"Are you in charge of everything?"

"No way. What do you think?" She smiles and looks down. She

follows a run in her tights with the tip of her finger. Then she shrugs.

"Help me, Alex. Try and remember. I need all the details you can give me. Tell me about his eyes. Not the shape or colour, tell me about the whites of his eyes. Were they yellow? Clear? Veined with red?"

I think about them. I try and relive the scene, like in a film. Him following me, him looking at me, him waiting for me. I close my eyes and project the scene inside my head, like at the cinema, but it feels more like a dream, like when you try and remember but the feelings are stronger than the images, and if you try and line them up accordingly, you lose them all.

"I don't know, white, I guess. I only saw him for a second."

"Were they the eyes of an old man or a young man? Sick or healthy? Your impression, Alex. What was your impression?"

"Young and healthy. Apart from the wound on his head."

"What wound?"

She sits up straight and looks at me carefully; I fumble for words.

"I did it to him." I touch my forehead. "With the door, when I slammed it against him. A cut, it was bleeding."

She gets up, walks around the room, chewing on the inside of her cheek, pushing at it with a finger as if she wanted to dig a hole through her cheek.

"Is that helpful to you?" I ask and she nods her head, yes.

"It's something," she says. "Something to put on the message board."

"What message board?"

"Never mind. Tell me about his voice, Alex. Deep, soft, high pitched?"

"I barely heard it. He was whispering."

"That's better. When someone whispers it's harder for them to disguise their voice. What did he say?"

She walks over to the bed and lowers the music. It fades away from the speakers. I look up at her; I'm a little embarrassed to have her so close by, without having showered, without having shaved, in my tracksuit bottoms, slippers and socks.

"He called my name. He said, 'Alessandro, open up, please.'" I'll never forget it. Like the first time I saw Profondo Rosso on TV. Like the first time I failed an exam. Like the first time Kristine whispered something naughty to me in Danish that I never discovered the meaning of.

She looks at the bed as if she wants to sit down, but there's not enough room between Dog and me. I move over a little, but she only rests her knee on the mattress, one hand on her thigh to stay balanced. She repeats my sentence in a low voice, with her eyes closed.

"His r: did he roll his rs? Were they sharp? What did they sound like?"

"I don't know: normal."

"His s: more of an sss or a shh sound?"

I close my eyes. I put a hand on my eyelids and try and pull out that voice from the darkness. I say his words to myself again, the way she did. Grazia moves my hand away, she picks up my chin and forces me to open my eyes.

"Don't repeat it the way you would say it. Try and hear it and say it to me the way he did."

"I don't know . . . the s, the s . . . he was whispering. Shit, I was scared!"

"I'm sorry."

Grazia gets up. She stands in front of the chair, she leans on it and chews at the inside of her cheek again. Her brow is furrowed as though she is thinking of something, her eyebrows so tightly knit they seem united. She's cute like that too. Thoughtful.

"What's the matter?" I say.

"I was thinking of something, but I forgot what it was. Doesn't matter. Keep talking . . . sooner or later it will come back."

"Why are you so interested in the voice?"

"Because it tells me a lot."

"How do you know?"

"Because it's my speciality. And because I live with a blind guy. He taught me to be sensitive to voices."

"Oh," I say.

Suddenly she brings her hand to her mouth in surprise. She opens her eyes really wide and murmurs: "Madonna!" And then louder, "Oh Madonna!"

"What's the matter?" I ask, but she doesn't answer. She takes her jacket off the chair and puts it on, looking at me without really seeing me. "What's the matter? Grazia, what's the matter?"

"Nothing," she says. "I remembered something I had been thinking about. Sorry, Alex, I have to go now. We'll talk more later, sorry."

She leaves the room before I can even get up. I hear her running down the stairs. There's something on the floor under the chair. I bend down and pick it up. It's her pregnancy test. I don't think it would be right to run after her. Anyway I already heard the door slam.

LICENCE TO CARRY FIREARMS FOR PERSONAL PROTECTION.
According to the regulations prescribed by TULS (Testo Unico Legge Sanitarie) in article 22 and in article 61 as well as those subsequent to it, the Prefetto can confer a licence on the following categories of individuals, should they require it:

– people who frequently carry valuables, including jewellery salesmen and employees who are entrusted with withdrawing and depositing large sums of cash

– people who have significant amounts of valuable goods in their shops, such as goldsmiths

– tradesmen who for reasons of business need to carry large sums of cash

– people who are considered to be at a high risk of kidnapping

– people who are exposed to particular aggressions or vendettas (legal counsel or taxidrivers, for example).

"We'll get him, sooner or later."

When Grazia left Alex's house she ran to her car and drove straight to the motorway. Between Ravenna and Bologna her idea came steadily into focus, until she was convinced it was the only possible explanation. Then, suddenly, it seemed stupid and all the air went out of her, leaving a sensation of emptiness and fatigue, like after a sleepless night. Then, slowly, the idea recomposed itself, filling her with growing enthusiasm.

Sometimes Pit Bull had used wax bullets and sometimes glass ones. Bullets that couldn't be traced. You couldn't trace the weapons that had fired them because there was no scratch on the bullets from the barrel. But he had used them only for some murders, in others, he wasn't even concerned about collecting the shells. He used the special untraceable bullets only in the region of Emilia Romagna. Why?

The application for a licence to carry a handgun or firearm should be presented on stamped paper to the Prefetto along with all relevant documentation, including a certification of psychological and physical wellbeing and one of instruction in the correct use and handling of a firearm, to be issued by the Tiro A Segno association (if military service was completed, then an autodeclaration is sufficient). Application must also include a declaration of residence, a certificate with names of family members and proof of having provided for the education of one's children and, in the case of those who have not performed their military service, a declaration attesting to the fact that this was not because he was a conscientious objector. Two photographs should be attached to the application, together with the receipt for 170,000 lire which must be paid to account number 8003, UFFICIO TASSE E CONCESSIONI GOVERNATIVE, ROMA, in addition to the sum of 4000 lire, which is to be paid to the Economato of the local Questura for the administrative cost of the permit.

"We'll get him, sooner or later."

As she drove down the motorway, Grazia went over everything in her mind as if answering the questions of Matera and Sarrina, not to mention those of Commissario Carlisi.

D'Orrico had told them why Pit Bull used special bullets. Pit Bull had tried to avoid any contact with the world of organised crime. He had tried to stay as clean as possible. He had used clean weapons, legally acquired at the armoury, officially declared and carried with the appropriate kind of licence from the Prefetto. He didn't need to find any clandestine rifle ranges or hidden places to train; he could go to the practise range and shoot any time he wished. When he killed someone outside of the region, he used normal bullets. He used special bullets only when he was closer to home, in order to widen the search area. It's easier to find all the people who have a Beretta or a Smith & Wesson in Bologna than to look for them all over Italy. He had used the special bullets three times: in Bologna, in Ferrara and in Rimini. Therefore, logic suggested, Pit Bull must live in the region of Emilia Romagna.

But why does he have a licence? Couldn't he buy the weapons in an armoury, declare them and then carry them illegally? Couldn't he simply have a licence to carry the weapons for sport and then carry the gun around unloaded, inside a holster? Yes . . .

Grazia went back over her thoughts and got so confused, she started tripping over the ends of sentences, repeating herself, losing her thread, stressing out. All right, she thought, let's add all the guns that people keep at home to the search list, as well as the sport licences.

"We'll get him, sooner or later."

What about bodyguards? And other military units? Since the Uno Bianca scandal nothing could be ruled out, theoretically at least. And what about the people who had seasonal licences for hunting? We have to count those, too.

"We'll get him, sooner or later."

We need to narrow down the field. By region: Emilia Romagna. Province of Bologna; Province of Ferrara; Reggio Emilia, Parma, Ravenna; Forlì; Rimini; Cesena? Is Cesena in the region of Emilia Romagna?

"We'll get him, sooner or later."

We need to narrow down the field by calibre and type of weapon. Which one? Maybe a .22, maybe a .40, maybe . . . what kind? Try and find a person who legally possesses a gun of any kind, of any calibre, anywhere in Emilia Romagna, with or without a licence. How many were there?

When she reached the toll booth in Bologna, Grazia had tears in her eyes. She seemed to get so close to Pit Bull, but then she'd lose him again. She saw him take shape, with the permit to carry a firearm, maybe as a jewellery salesman, and then suddenly he had transformed into a bodyguard, a goldsmith, a taxi driver. A policeman. She clenched her teeth, the way she used to when she was little, when the other children in her junior school in southern Italy teased her for being the smallest. Everyone would stand around her: Di Corato, Puglisi, Naccari, all of them waiting for her, ready to whistle at her. She sat inside the car after she had parked it in the piazza in front of the Questura and breathed deeply for a minute. Then she lowered her head, clenched her teeth, said "fuck you" to herself and got out. When she got upstairs to Carlisi's office she had already put together a few different speeches. She was as obstinate and stubborn as ever. Her enthusiasm hadn't returned, but maybe she didn't really need that after all.

"We'll get him, Grazia. Sooner or later. It's not a bad idea . . . we have to sit down, gather the data and sift through it," the commissioner had said, nodding and leaning back in his armchair. He locked his hands behind his neck and nodded again. "Yes, there is a chance. Sooner or later, we'll get him."

"But when, Dottore? We have to move quickly. How do you explain the thing with D'Orrico? Why did he save him? Why does he leave pictures of pit bulls everywhere? Dottore, this guy has a plan. He has an idea. It's imperative that we catch him immediately."

"We'll get him, Grazia. We always do." That's what he said to her.

Grazia went back into her office and wept tears of frustration.

Stress, she thought to herself. Damn it. She put her hand in her pocket to look for the pregnancy test and found only the gun. Fuck, she thought, it would have been better if I had lost the gun.

She went up to the message board and tore off all the Post-its that weren't conclusive, the ones with banalities on them, like "professional killer". She removed all the ones that had to do with long investigations that she couldn't carry out personally, like the one about money. Only two remained.

HE LIVES IN EMILIA ROMAGNA.

HE HAS A CUT ON HIS FOREHEAD.

With neither desperation nor anger, but with the cold sensation of someone who feels as though they have been taken for a fool and then reaches the rational conclusion that they can't do anything about it, at least for the time being, Grazia tore off the photograph of the pit bull that was attached to the board and screwed it up.

At that very moment, Sarrina came in.

"Grazia . . . Can you come here? There's a fellow who wants to see you."

HE HAD A COP'S SAD FACE: LONG AND NARROW, WITH grey bags under his eyes and a pointed nose. He was wearing an overcoat that was too heavy for the season; he was tall and balding.

"Carrone," he said, standing up to introduce himself and shaking Grazia's hand. He bowed his head slightly and tapped his heels together. He took out a business card, identical to the one that Carlisi had on his desk and handed it to her. It read MARCO CARRONE. PRIVATE INVESTIGATIONS and then, underneath, RETIRED MARSHAL OF THE ARMED FORCES. EXPERIENCED INVESTIGATOR. It was one of those business cards that you can have made by a machine at a motorway service station.

"I was actually a brigadiere," he said, "but I would have become maresciallo when they retired me."

Grazia sat down on the edge of the commissioner's desk. He was busy begging forgiveness from Carrone for abandoning him in a *pensione* in Bologna for two days until he himself came back to the Questura to say, "Well, if there's no need for me, I guess I'll be going." Carrone shook his head, his eyes half closed, a slight grimace on his cop's face, as if he was used to being forgotten. Then he bent down and took a notebook out of his typical cop's bag that he had rested on the seat of the chair. He placed the notebook on Carlisi's desk. Grazia leaned over to see what it was, thinking she'd have to read it, but Carrone suddenly put his hands together and looked as though he was getting ready to talk. He turned his gaze to her, maybe only because she was standing in front of him, but it seemed like she was the one to whom he wanted to tell his story.

"I'm taking this down," he had said to that burnt remainder of a man at the scene of the crash. He had written quickly, leaving space at the top for the initial formalities, "Before me, Brigadiere Carrone Marco . . ." etc. He wrote down everything that the man spat into his ear. The saliva and blood sprayed against his cheek. When he couldn't quite understand, he took a deep breath to withstand the strong smell of burnt flesh and got a little closer. The man spoke for less than a minute and howled like a wounded dog when one of the ambulance attendants tried to carry him away.

A few broken sentences came from his burnt throat in a scratchy gurgle – Carrone wrote them all down, verbatim. Afterwards, before he let the attendants take the stretcher away, he had signed his notes and made the attendants do the same, as witnesses.

"The man died on his way to the hospital because of loss of blood; the authorities denounced me for interfering with emergency assistance," he said. "The Unit didn't cover for me and they kicked me out. What do you think, Dottore, was I wrong to do it?"

"Well," said Carlisi, shrugging. "That's not the point. Please continue, Brigadiere."

He couldn't quite accept the fact that they had dumped him. He couldn't accept the fact that they didn't care about his notes, which he had gathered with so much precision and care. So he continued his research on his own, with fewer resources, naturally, because he was only a private investigator, even if he did have years of experience. He still had a few friends in the Armed Forces, though, and they helped him answer a few of his questions.

The man who was driving the car that had exploded was a colonel in the Air Force who worked for Secret Services. No-one ever discovered why they had planted a bomb in his car, but that was only a detail.

"As he was dying, the colonello told me that the person who planted the bomb in his car was a professional killer named Pit Bull."

Grazia leaned forward.

"He said that Pit Bull wanted to kill him because he knew who he was. It was something to do with weapons and murders committed for the Service. I didn't understand, the words didn't mean anything to me."

Grazia nodded, making a gesture that he should continue his story.

"He told me that Pit Bull belonged to someone. Yes, that's right, that he belonged to someone, and that this someone was Don Masino Barletta. And that Pit Bull had killed him too."

Grazia looked at the commissioner, a little baffled. Something didn't make sense, she felt confused. She looked to him for some further information to help her focus. The name Barletta rang a bell, but she couldn't put her finger on precisely why.

Matera went to speak, but the commissioner made a sign for him to be quiet. It was Brigadiere Carrone's time to be heard; this was his chance to tell the whole story.

"Don Masino Tommaso Barletta was a minor Mafia figure. In 1979 he was arrested and then sent away from Palermo under house arrest. His case was later reviewed, but he never went back to Sicily. Apparently he never did anything else: didn't check on anything, didn't control anything, didn't deal in anything. By 1981 his name was respected again among the clans, both the stronger and the weaker ones. Word got out that he provided killers to those who needed them. In 1995 he disappeared from the scene altogether."

"I get it," Grazia said. "Don Masino was one of Pit Bull's procurators, like D'Orrico. Well, this is a step forward."

"There's more to it," Carlisi said. "You know where they sent Don Masino? You tell them, Brigadiere, it's your story."

Carrone nodded, and for a moment his cop's face seemed a fraction less sad.

"House arrest in Budrio, in the province of Bologna." He rested his notebook on the table and slid it over towards Grazia, close enough for her to see the red halos on its cover where the brigadier had scraped off spots of dried, caked blood.

"It's all here," Carrone said. "The colonello's words as well as my investigations on Don Masino. Sworn to and signed."

NARROW IT DOWN. CONNECT. RULE OUT CERTAIN possibilities. Narrow it down further still.

We know Pit Bull is in Emilia Romagna. Don Masino lived in Budrio in Emilia Romagna, on via Wagner, 10. First connection.

Narrow it down: get the list of all those living in Bologna and province who own firearms. Get a record of gun sales and owners' licence applications. The list goes from Accorsi, Michele to Zarrillo, Elena. Too many.

Narrow it down further still. Add a Post-it next to the other two. They're her intuitions, only intuitions, but they're almost certain. Narrow it down further still.

Get the list of those who have a licence to carry a weapon in the province of Bologna. Eliminate those who own weapons, but keep them at home, under lock and key, with the ammunition hidden away from their children. Only look at those who carry a pistol on them, in a holster. People with a wide variety of guns, preferably a .22 and a .40. The list goes from Bonetti, Marco to Tibaldi, Francesco.

Narrow it down further still: one more Post-it on the board. What once looked like a straight line is now beginning to resemble a circle.

Grazia's intuition: he holds a job that allows him to justify his movements and manage his own schedule. Private investigators, financiers, company owners, representatives of businesses with precious samples: the list goes from Carletti, Piero to Quadalti, Mariano. Getting better.

Narrow it down further still. Add another Post-it. Getting warmer.

Intuition: he dresses up, like an actor; he transforms himself, like an actor; he recites a part, like an actor. Find all the people who hold licences to carry firearms who have also taken acting, diction and make-up classes. No list available. Would have to gather information from all the theatres, cultural associations, community centres, acting groups ... too complicated. That Post-it goes further down, lower, just in case.

Reconnect. The list from Carletti to Quadalti on one side. Don Masino on the other.

Someone knocks on the door and Grazia raises her head. It's an agent in uniform, with a package in his hand. "It's for you, Ispettore. A kid brought it."

"What kind of kid? Never mind, it doesn't matter. Anyway if it was Pit Bull, he could be anywhere by now."

The package is square, covered in wrapping paper and tied with red ribbon that spouts up in two curly fountains. What if it explodes in her hand? What if it's someone's ear? Or if it's a bullet with her name on it?

Grazia opened it. She guessed what it was as she was opening it. She could tell from the two curls of ribbon, torn a little bit on the edge because the scissors had been held clumsily. It wasn't perfect enough for Pit Bull.

It was the pregnancy test she had dropped at Alex's house.

She put it down on the table next to the computer. Back to the board, this time with the list in her hand.

Carletti, Piero; Castelli, Silvio; Costa, Daniele; Davito, Alessandro; Emaldi, Pietro; Facchini, Primo; Foret, Gaetano; Franchini, Giulio; Iotti, Lisa; Lombardini, Alessandro; Marchini, Vittorio.

Marchini, Vittorio.

Salesman. Single owner and administrator of a small import and distribution jewellery company.

Marchini, Vittorio.

Holder of a licence to carry firearms for personal defence. Holder of an automatic Glock 23 .40 S&W, a Sig Sauer P229 .40 and an automatic sport Beretta 71, .22.

Marchini, Vittorio.

Residence: via Wagner, 12, 40054 Budrio.

THEY WERE WATCHING HER THROUGH A SLIT IN THE side of the van. Sarrina had to press himself up against it to see her clearly; closing one eye, he had to push his cheek against the corner of the aperture and then slide over to the other side of the slit to follow her with the other eye as she moved. It wasn't easy. Via Wagner was a dead end. It curved at a right angle and both lengths of the street were of equal width, wide and clean. It was a typical short residential street. On one side of the road there was a row of houses that all looked the same: each had two floors plus an attic, a garden and a garage. On the other side of the street was a row of trees, and then open fields. Number 12 was at the end of the road. They hadn't been able to park any closer because there were no unoccupied spaces. They couldn't park in front of the house because a Volvo estate car was in front of the wooden post that separated the dead end from the small public park that was at the end of the road. The only thing they could do was to squeeze the van into a space halfway down the street, and they were able to do that only because Matera had rung the bell of a few of the houses, found the owner of one of the cars and made him move it. From where they were, Matera, Sarrina and two agents from the Mobile Unit with machine guns and bulletproof vests were just able to watch Grazia as she walked down the street.

Grazia had come in a car with Dottore Carlisi; he parked around the corner. She walked towards the house at a steady gait and with a glossy magazine in her hand, her bomber jacket zipped up to her neck to hide her bulletproof vest. She stopped at number 12, leaned on the gatepost and read the name on the bell. "Marchini". She rang the bell.

She was sweating. She wished it was her gun she was holding alongside her thigh and not a magazine, but if Signora Marchini had seen it, she never would have opened the door. And if *he* saw her, she'd be dead.

"Yes, can I help you?"

Grazia waved the magazine at the lady standing in the doorway at the end of the path. She pushed on the gate but it was locked.

"Hello, is Vittorio home?"

He never parked his car in front of the house, always at the back, on the road behind the house, and then walked down the path that separated his house from the park. There was really no reason to do it that way; it wasn't for security. It was just because there were never any parking spaces on via Wagner. When he heard her voice he was behind the hedge, out of sight.

"Hello, is Vittorio home?"

The lady held up her hand to shield her eyes from the sun that shone down through the branches. It was a strange autumn, it had lasted a long time and the winter seemed like it would never come, there had been only a few cold days that felt like January. Better that way.

"No, he's at work. Who are you?"

"I'm a friend of Vittorio's. From work. I have to leave something for him."

Vittorio continued walking, but instead of turning to the right, towards the house, he turned left into the park. He turned away from his street and went on until he found a tree that he could hide behind. He bent down as if to tie his shoe, with one knee on the grass, and he looked at the garden.

She was dark-haired and not particularly tall. She had an olive green bomber jacket and a magazine in her hand.

Thought: I don't know her.

"I'm a friend of Vittorio's. From work. I have to leave something for him."

Grazia gesticulated with the magazine again and pushed at the grey metal gate, coated with anti-rust paint. The lady took a step back in the doorway, carefully, so she wouldn't trip. She slid an arm round the corner and clicked the gate open.

Vittorio's mother waited for Grazia at the door with a curious smile on her face. She was wearing a pinny and a blue cardigan that she had bought at the market, with a small heart sewn on to its front. Usually she wore a jumper too, but she didn't want to be too warm while she was ironing.

"Who is this pretty young girl?" she asked when Grazia came up close. She was glad because it was nice to see the pretty face of a young woman, but she was also wary and suspicious because Vittorio already had a girlfriend, Annalisa, and it was serious. Careful now.

"Are you sure your son's not home?"

Thought: I might be wrong.

She might not be a cop. She could be selling a subscription to a magazine. For watches, jewellery. A new car. Maybe she's here for a bill. The union.

He looked at the girl standing next to his mother. Trainers and jeans, narrow at the ankle. A bomber jacket that was roomy on the shoulders. Careful: she looks stronger than her face lets on. She has a Mediterranean physique; petite, athletic. It's a possibility. Something was sticking out of her left pocket. The tip of something with a black loop around it. Was it a camera? Binoculars? A pair of gloves? Maybe. He watched how she moved her hands. One hung down by her side, holding the magazine. The other one was held up near her waist, closed in a fist. Was she nervous? No. At ease? No. She stood with her head at an angle, as if she was looking inside, behind his mother.

He looked down the road. Empty cars, he recognised them all, they belonged to the neighbours. There was a van he didn't recognise, but then he didn't really spend much time at home.

Thought: he might be wrong.

It all depended on her next move.

"Are you sure your son's not at home?"

Vittorio's mother pursed her lips and scrutinised her visitor, the way a dog might look at a stranger. Suddenly, that cordial and careful smile became suspicious.

"Yes, why?"

"Police, signora. Ispettore Negro. We have to come in."

Thought: so, this is it.

He got up from next to the tree and moved behind the trunk to watch. He saw the girl pull at the strap sticking out of her pocket and take out a walkie-talkie. He saw her bring it to her mouth, press the side button and say "Action!" almost in a whisper. Then he watched as she held out her arm in front of his mother, pushing her away without touching her.

So, he thought. This is how it is.

From where he was behind the tree he could have extracted his Glock from its holster, got into position, his right wrist leaning against the tree, left hand steadying his right. He would have shot quickly in a horizontal line, from left to right, first shooting at the heavy guy, who was now halfway down the path, then at the younger one at the gate and then at the other two coming down the road. He would have shot them in the head or in the legs, but not in the torso, because of their vests. He would have shot three steps ahead of them. Another two shots in the chest of the man in jacket and tie who was already on the path. One shot in the head of the girl with the bomber jacket, being careful not to hit his mother. With whatever ammunition was left he would have finished off the men who were already on the ground.

But he didn't do any of this.

So, he thought. This is how it is.

He turned his back on the house and walked to where he had parked his car.

SHE DIDN'T UNDERSTAND WHAT WAS GOING ON AND probably never would. She looked at all the people coming in and going up and down the stairs and kept repeating, "Is it because of the weapons? Vittorio has a permit, you know. He can carry them, he's a jewellery salesman." And when someone said, "Dottore, would you come up here for a minute?" and she tried to go, too, the girl held her back and asked, "Do you have a photograph of Vittorio you could show me? It's possible this is all a mistake . . ."

Of course it was a mistake. They were all making a mistake. All she had to do was show them a photograph.

"This is Vittorio when he was 20. He's good looking, isn't he? But remember, he has a girlfriend."

Grazia took the photographs that the signora had pulled out of a shoe box. There were several of them, all neatly stacked, some in black and white, others with serrated edges, as they had in the 50s, others were small and square and with faded colours, the date printed on the side in small characters: August 2, 1962; September 15, 1978. There were even some faded Polaroids and a small wedding album.

"We don't take a lot of pictures," the signora had said. "And Vittorio never liked having his picture taken."

Grazia looked at the photos. There was one, a shiny rectangular one, in which the figure seemed to be in relief. It was a portrait shot of Vittorio, taken while he was talking to someone whose blurred arm was barely visible. Vittorio wasn't in focus either, but you could see him. He had a straight nose and even lineaments; he was reasonably good looking. His hair was very short. He had redeye from the flash. One of his hands was at his chin, a finger resting on his lips as though he was listening carefully. Twenty years old. 1990. Definitely not the look of a killer. Grazia knew what killers looked like, she had studied their photographs, she had seen them at rest, she had held a gun to them, she had looked them in the eyes as she handcuffed them. This man did not have the look of a killer. Not yet, anyway.

"Would you happen to have a more recent one?" she asked.

The signora sighed and looked in the box. She dragged her finger across the pictures and shook her head.

"I don't think so. You have to catch him off guard; he always has an excuse. He was shy as a boy, a little introverted. But he was good, you know what I mean? As good as gold. Here's a picture from last year. It's from his passport."

A colour photograph. As bland as any document photograph. Vittorio was in the foreground, he stared dead ahead, his gaze serious and stern, staring at something that wasn't there. He had very short dark hair, his mouth was shut, his lips were full though not big, and his eyes . . . Grazia brought the picture up close and then held it away from her, concentrating on it to make out the colour of his eyes. They seemed light, maybe green. It wasn't important, she would have found out that kind of information from his file: eye colour, height and weight. She would have liked to see more photographs. Some that revealed his expression or personality. But instead, nothing. No discernible look of a killer. He was as blank as an identikit.

"If you don't mind, we'll keep these, just to see if we're making a mistake."

Vittorio's mother nodded in a way that suggested she wasn't

even listening. She was smiling, looking at a photograph in black and white with rounded edges, which she held with both her hands so as not to put her fingers on it.

"This is the one I like best," she said, and passed it to Grazia.

He was a child. A ten-year-old boy. He was on his knees, huddled over something that disappeared below the lower edge of the photograph. He rested his elbows on his knees and held his chin in his hands. He was in a field. The grass looked smooth and soft, like an ocean. It must have been taken in the park behind via Wagner because you could see the house, even though it was slightly out of focus. The child had straight hair, it was cut slightly above his ears and parted down the middle. A lock of hair fell casually over his eyes. It must have been windy. And sunny, too, because he was squinting. He wanted to keep his eyes open. They held an enigmatic expression. Not strange, just enigmatic. Difficult to understand, revealing neither melancholy nor enthusiasm. He was waiting. His face showed the hint of a smile, but not a genuine smile. The corner of his mouth was raised, as if someone was telling him a funny story, but he was waiting to hear the end before deciding whether to smile or not. He was a good-looking child, Grazia thought, and she told his mother so.

"Yes, he was," she replied, "and so talkative, too. How he talked! Here he looks serious because he had just . . ."

She interrupted herself, shaking her head as if brushing away a fly. She sighed.

"What?" Grazia asked. "What happened?"

Vittorio's mother shook her head. "Nothing," she mumbled, but her voice broke. She began to cough and tried to take the photo back from Grazia, who held on to it tightly and pressed it against her chest.

"What did he have? Was he sick? Did he have an accident?"

The signora kept coughing, as if trying to cover the sound of

Grazia's words. At the same time she shook her head and waved her finger, no. Grazia raised her voice, and almost shouted.

"What happened, signora? What happened to your son when he was ten?"

WHEN VITTORIO WAS TEN HE KILLED A CHILD. IT WAS an accident. It happened at school. He was still at junior school at the time.

Grazia reconstructed the story by interrogating the teacher and the social workers. She had gone all the way to Milan, to the scene of Vittorio's first crime, to put the pieces of the puzzle together. Vittorio's mother didn't tell her anything new. Neither did Annalisa. When Grazia introduced herself to Annalisa in the library in Ferrara, her face said it all. When she said she was from the police and that she was there to talk about Vittorio, Annalisa covered her mouth with her hands.

"Oh my God, did something happen to him?"

Annalisa leaned back on the desk in her librarian's office when Grazia explained the reason for her visit.

"Wait, wait, wait, Ispettore . . . What was your name?"

"Negro."

"Wait a minute, Ispettore Negro. You're telling me that the man I have been going out with for the past two years is a professional killer and that he has killed how many people?"

Dottore Carlisi and Di Cara laughed when Grazia told them about her visit to Annalisa. They wouldn't stop laughing. Even Matera smiled. Sarrina wasn't there: he was parking the car that he had used to pick up Di Cara from the airport.

The family had been living in Milan at the time. Every morning his mother took him to school and every afternoon she picked him up. He could have gone to school alone – they lived nearby and Vittorio was a sensible and intelligent child. When he did make the journey alone, if his mother wasn't well and his father had already left for work, he'd put his jacket over his smock and zip it all the way up, take his backpack and leave. He always took the longer route but he got to school in time just the same; he always ran the last part of the way. His house was near via Paolo Sarpi and he liked to cut through the Chinese neighbourhood. He liked to look at the Chinese people and try to understand what they were thinking, what they wanted to say when they opened their eyes really wide, or when they frowned and shook their heads. He stopped in front of shops and looked in until they noticed him. Then he'd run off to school. The teachers were relatively satisfied with his work. Relatively. Vittorio was a decent student, he studied, he applied himself, but he was a strange child. No, not strange. Difficult. He didn't speak much and he didn't play with other children. He rarely laughed and if he did it was really no more than a smile. He didn't mind when his teachers got angry with him, he would take it in silence, staring at the ground, but then, on occasion and without reason, he'd lose control. He never shouted or yelled, but he'd lose control physically. He'd throw things on the ground or against the wall. Once he even pushed over a desk. It didn't happen often, but the few times it did were enough for the teachers to request psychological assistance. Vittorio was a child with behavioural problems.

Sarrina arrived, making some noise as he came in. Matera had to get up to hold the door for him. Grazia took the opportunity to stop and think about her message board for a minute and the photograph of the child in the middle of an ocean of grass. The photograph kept falling down, it was hanging on by only half a Post-it note. She had tried reattaching it, pushing hard against the Post-it, which had lost all its stick, until she realised that there were small, round magnets at the bottom of the board, like mini draughts pieces. She put one on each corner of the photo and straightened it: a ten-year-old child smiled into the camera, his hands under his chin.

His parents chose to keep their son at school until 5.00. He didn't seem to mind. He read, drew, played games or football in the courtyard, but always alone. He'd bounce the ball against the wall, over and over again, barely even moving. At home he did the same kinds of thing. He watched television. The psychologist had recommended that he spend time with other children, so his mother signed him up for swimming lessons. She took him there after school and another mother brought him home. Vittorio's mother didn't know that her son participated only in the first half of his swimming lesson. When it was time for his team to play water volleyball he'd invent an excuse and say he didn't feel well. He'd get out of the water and sit and watch. His mother couldn't stay with him at the pool because by then his father's attacks had already begun.

"Are you giving us the sob story, Negro?" Dottore Carlisi asked. "You're not siding with Pit Bull are you?"

Grazia blushed violently. She felt her face turn red all the way to the roots of her hair. She answered more forcefully than necessary.

"It's all part of the data, Dottore. I don't want to sympathise with Pit Bull, I want to get him."

She started in again. At school, in the dinner hall, there was a child from another class who didn't like Vittorio. When they were at the table, before they began to eat, all the children rushed to see which plate they'd been given as each one had a different animal on it. They'd shout and scream even after the pasta had arrived, raising their plates in the air and yelling out things like, "Whoever has the horse gets to play with me! Whoever has the elephant gets to play with me!" Everyone would do it except for Vittorio, who put his napkin over his plate. The other children always teased him about this. One of the children, who was much bigger than the others, would yank on Vittorio's backpack, push him against the wall, or smack the back of his head when he passed him in the courtyard or in the corridor. Vittorio never said anything. He never reacted. Until one day, when he pushed him through a glass partition. The glass broke and a shard of it sliced through the boy's jugular.

Dottore Carlisi didn't say a word. No-one did. Di Cara murmured, "An accident?" and ran his finger over the seal of the Direzione Investigative Anitmafia, Palermo that was printed on the file in front of him. He seemed tense.

It had been an accident. There were problems, accusations, legal provisions, but Vittorio was only ten. He was a child. It was deemed an accident. The Marchini's paid a sum of money to the victim's family and the story was kept out of the papers. Vittorio was calm about it; he blocked the whole thing out, as if nothing had happened. The court psychiatrist suggested they move, that they get a change of scenery. Vittorio's mother was originally from Budrio, near Bologna, so they moved there, to a quiet villa on via Wagner, 12. And that's where they met Don Masino.

Di Cara raised his hand, like a student at school, and then patted the file in front of him.

"Now let me tell you what I've got," he said. "Two unusual murder cases, one in Palermo and the other in Florence. In Palermo, in 1981, a minor boss named Peppino Cannata was killed. Peppino liked a place called Il castello dell'Emiro. It's one of the poorest neighbourhoods in Palermo, but he was born there and he went there as often as he could. To think, to meditate, let's say. Peppino wasn't easy to knock off because he was always armed and he never trusted anyone. Don Masino had a score to settle with Peppino, but no-one in Palermo wanted to do him the favour, even if Peppino was a pain in the arse for a lot of people.

It was impossible to plan a surprise attack and pull off something clean, and no-one wanted a massacre."

Di Cara raised a finger in the air, as if to be sure of holding their attention while he took a breath.

"The circumstances surrounding the murder that took place in Florence were similar to the ones in Palermo. It was . . . 1982," he said, quickly checking the file. "The victim was a Lebanese man, someone connected with the Secret Service. He was in a hotel surrounded by bodyguards so that no-one could get close to him. Sure, they could have killed him by shooting a missile at his window or he could have been gunned down by a machine gun in the reception room, but no-one wanted that kind of publicity. Anyway, both Cannata and the Lebanese man were killed. Both jobs were done neatly: four shots with a 6.35 in the head. And guess what the murders have in common? Witness reports from both cases mention the presence of a child."

HE COULDN'T SLEEP ON HIS SIDE ANY MORE. FOR YEARS he had slept in exactly the same position: on his stomach, with one arm under the pillow and the other folded on top, but now he couldn't do it any more. His shoulder would begin to ache and his hand would start to go numb, as if the blood got blocked in his veins. He had to turn over continually, from one side to the other. He turned over onto his back, locked his fingers behind his neck and looked up at the roof of the camper van. He wondered how certain mental associations took place. He had been thinking about his father and suddenly Don Masino came to mind.

He had been thinking about his father in the retirement home, sitting on that powder-blue chair. It occurred to him that he may never see him again. Then, suddenly, in his place, he visualised Don Masino. There was no physical resemblance (Don Masino was small and fidgety, and he pictured him somewhere else, doing something entirely different). First he saw his father and then he saw Don Masino, as if in a dream.

Thought: the first time I saw him.

The first time he saw him was shortly after their arrival in Budrio. Don Masino knew what had happened. He knew everything about everybody. Vittorio looked at him standing in the doorway talking to his father. He looked ancient but was probably no more than 50. More than anything else Vittorio remembered the light. It could have been a forced memory, like something he had seen in a film, but there was a bright white light which blurred the edges and created long shadows all the way down into the living room. The old man, who was wearing a yellow Lacoste polo shirt, took a step forward into the house and smiled at him. You must be Vittorio. He bent down to shake his hand and looked him straight in the eye. He looked at him deeply, as if he were searching for something. When Don Masino smiled Vittorio knew that he understood that Vittorio's crime was no accident.

He couldn't lie on his back any more. His fingers had gone numb, bent like that behind his neck. He needed to roll over again. He tried to stay where he was, but he moved his hands onto his stomach, his fingers interlocking so that his arms wouldn't slide down to his sides. He knew instantly that he wouldn't last long in that position. Outside, somewhere in the car park, he heard the noise of a lorry passing by.

But the memory of the two men standing at the door wasn't the link between his father and Don Masino. It wasn't because of that moment that he imagined them together. Even if he tried to concentrate the true motive wouldn't come to mind, not immediately anyway. The image of his father faded; now there was only the other one, the little, aged-looking man with the yellow Lacoste shirt.

Thought: in the countryside.

In Sicily he must have dressed differently, but in Budrio he always dressed the same way, in that yellow shirt. His memories seemed to be growing increasingly similar to his dreams: absurd and surreal. He was walking with the old man along the bank of a canal. What he liked about Don Masino was that he talked constantly. No, not Don Masino: he didn't want to be called that. He wanted to be called uncle Tommaso. Zio Tommaso. Zio Tommaso. He had to repeat it to himself a few times. Zio Tommaso. His tongue moved inside his closed mouth. It didn't sound right, it took concentration, and it interrupted the flow of memories, so he stopped. Don Masino. Don Masino talked. Vittorio didn't ask questions. He liked to listen. They walked through the fields, Vittorio stepping on the clods of earth. They walked through the vineyards, Vittorio walking under the arbours. They walked all the way to the bridge over the river. Don Masino would be talking the whole time and he would be listening and watching. He didn't remember everything Don Masino said. If he had to reconstruct his speeches, as if they had been scripted, with the same punchlines and intonation, he wouldn't be able to do it. But he hadn't forgotten what he had said – he kept it inside him like a feeling, a thought that he could neither see nor articulate. Don Masino talked about what Vittorio did at school, about the boy he had killed.

He heard a noise outside the window. It was the voice of someone walking past. It was closer than the other voices had been up until then. He raised himself up on an elbow, slid a hand under the bed and took out his Beretta, pointing it at the door of the camper van. He raised the lever with his thumb and aimed the silencer through the cross hairs. The voice had already faded, it was now as indistinct as the other voices in the car park of the service station. But he continued to hold the gun there anyway.

Thought: his hand.

His hand had been too small to hold a real gun. He was only ten years old. His hand was still that of a child, with short fingers, a narrow palm and a small, soft thumb. Don Masino had found him a special gun, a Baby Mauser 6.35 calibre modified with an addition on the handle so that he could slide his hand in, like a glove. He remembered the pain in his wrist at first and how it lessened with each training session. He remembered how proud he was when he managed to get to the end of the charger without stopping to lower his arm. Don Masino's method was based on developing the will and on encouraging pleasure taken in a job well done. He understood it only much later. He had been too young at the time.

His hand began to tremble a little. He could see it from the tip of the silencer. He bent his wrist slightly to the left. That stopped the trembling.

Thought: il castello dell'Elmiro.

He could see the place in front of him, as if watching a film from his youth: the voices, the noises, the movements, with mental changes in focus and close ups that he added on as he remembered it; the memory was clearer even than the real event. Il castello dell'Elmiro, Don Masino had explained to him on the plane, wasn't really a castle. He didn't want him to think that his assignment was some kind of fable or fairy story. It was a job, a job that needed to be done well, in the same way his mother might ask him to clean up his room or help hang up the sheets. It wasn't a game, it was a job that needed to be done, and only he could do it. Il castello dell'Emiro was an old Arab fortress of which only the walls remained. Built around it, inside it and on the hillside above it were small illegal ramshackle homes made of stone and cement. Cannata was sitting on a large boulder, smoking. Vittorio walked up to him with one hand in the pocket of his jacket and the other one holding on to the strap of his rucksack, which contained a few notebooks. He stopped in front of Cannata, took out his 6.35 and shot him in the face four times. Then he ran back down the roads that he had studied to the place where Don Masino was waiting for him in a car.

He couldn't hold the silencer steady any more. He lowered the lever with his thumb and put the .22 back under the bed. It was a stupid exercise – if he couldn't have held it steady with one hand he would simply have used two. He turned over on his side and pulled his legs up, slipping his hands between his thighs the way he used to when he was a child, when it started getting colder at night, or when he had a temperature.

Thought: they were happy that I got along with Don Masino.

Thought: Don Masino's voice; like a pit bull that's trained to kill.

Thought: (vision) his father at the window, behind the curtain, as white as a ghost, watching as 20-year-old Vittorio shoved Don Masino's legs into the boot of the car.

Thought: his father's gaze, his father's terror, his father, looking down at him from the window.

That was the link. That was the mental association between his father and Don Masino. But by now the memory had vanished. He slipped his arm under the pillow and stretched out his legs, hoping to fall asleep before he needed to roll over again.

SHE COULDN'T EVEN FIGURE OUT HOW TO USE THAT damn test properly. The instructions said to urinate into the container and dip the swab in. But it wasn't clear how the results should be interpreted and she didn't want to panic over nothing. So she poured out the small plastic cup that she had filled with urine, splashing her hand as she did so, and threw it into the sanitary towel diposal bin. She put the swab back in the box and returned to her office.

While she was walking down the corridor it occurred to her that most people usually have a friend or a mother who knows about these things. She didn't have any close female friends and her mother was in Puglia, in Nardò. If she had called, her mother would have been on her way to Bologna with all their relatives before Grazia could even hang up the phone. On the threshold of her office, she ran into Sarrina. She had to slip the test behind her back so he wouldn't see it or he'd only have a dig at her over it.

On the magnetic board remained the photograph of the child in the middle of the ocean of grass. All the Post-its were in the bin. Now wasn't the time to ask who he was, where he hid his money, how he got his weapons. Now they had to catch him. Look for him, find him, catch him.

Spread out on the camp bed were recordings of the telephone conversations between via Wagner and Annalisa in Ferrara, between Budrio and Milano and all the numbers included in the agenda belonging to Marchini Jewels (which were very few).

Catch him if he talks to someone.

On the floor, under the table and against the wall were rolls of fax paper directed to all the Questure with the names of (almost) all the hotels, bed and breakfasts, *pensione* and hostels in Italy.

Catch him if he checks into a hotel anywhere.

On the table were copies of photograms sent to the Questure and the Police Commissioners, to the commanders of the Carabinieri stations, to the police barracks, to the Polstrada, to the Polaria and to the Capitaneria del Porto.

Catch him if he tries to leave the country.

Catch him if he uses his documents, if he pays for anything with a debit or credit card, if he tries to withdraw money from the San Marino banks, if he uses his telepass or if he drives around in his car. Catch him if he uses his mobile phone with the phone card (no: that would be too stupid) or with a stolen card (yes, that one) because he probably doesn't know that even mobile phones, not just the SIM card, have an identification number inside them and if he turns it on, even for a second, he will be connected to a radio link and will be traced.

In a pile on the chair are the first ballistic reports for the weapons found in Budrio and San Marino. Two positive matches. Then the 16 declared by D'Orrico. Total number of murders: 18.

On the computer was a psychiatric report by Professor Morris which he had sent by e-mail to Dottore Carlisi with a copy to Grazia.

SUBJECT: VITTORIO MARCHINI, AKA PIT BULL. *One must take into consideration that ever since the age of ten, Marchini has planned killings; he has subordinated his life to this activity. The fact that as of 1999 he has signed some of his murders, revealing his existence and linking the crimes, should be interpreted as an intensification of the psychotic process. On one hand, the subject is looking for a form of expression that will let him get out of the silence in which he has been mired these many years, on the other, it is a call for help: Marchini feels like he is on the edge of the abyss and wants to be rescued before he falls into it.*

"Bullshit," reads a comment from the commissioner at the end of the report.

The photograph on the message board – of the child in the sea of grass – was obliterated by the sunlight streaming through the window, open in order to get some much needed fresh air. It seemed as though the child in the picture was no longer there, as though the photograph had been taken out of the acid bath too soon and the image had disappeared. Grazia moved the shutters so the photograph was no longer in the direct glare and the child returned to the middle of the ocean of grass.

Catch him when he makes a move.

Sarrina stepped back into the doorway.

Grazia left the Questura, zipping her bomber jacket all the way up. It was getting cold. Sarrina asked if she wanted a lift but she shook her head: no thank you, I'll walk home. Come on, it's going to rain, I'll take you to the bus stop. Okay, she said, even though she knew it was a mistake. She wanted to be alone.

"I saw that box in your hand. Anything to tell us?"

"Don't be dumb. I still have to take the test. Anyway, I don't think I'm pregnant."

"How late are you?"

"More than a week."

"Christ . . ."

"Come on, Sarrina! What the hell do you know? You don't know the first thing about this kind of stuff!"

"If you're pregnant, will you keep it?"

"I don't know."

"But are you?"

"I don't know, I don't know! I don't know!"

She got out of the car at the bus stop and slammed the door.

Sarrina was right. She pulled down her jacket to cover her holster, shoved her hands into her pockets and walked towards the piazza. The air was damp. It smelled like something had burnt, like iron. Sooner or later it was going to rain.

She sat at the back of the bus, near the door, sideways in her seat with her legs dangling over the steps. She leaned on the metal bar, rested her chin on her fist and closed her eyes. She was exhausted. She fell asleep, only for a few seconds, blanked out in a fizzy, disconnected whiteness. She came undone, turned off. The first jolt of the bus jarred her awake, sweating and with a dry mouth, as if she had been asleep for hours, but now she felt even more tired than before. She was glad she hadn't dreamed because, if she had, she would certainly have dreamt of him, of the child in the photograph. A ten-year-old boy trained by a Mafia boss to kill like a fighting dog. She was going home to try and forget about it, yet here she was thinking of it again.

To get her mind off the case she put her hand in her pocket and touched the pregnancy test. That's why the young boy was so much on her mind, she thought. As soon as I get home, I'll do it. But away from Simone. I'll hide it. Why? Because it's my own thing.

She raised her eyes up to the window and saw the stripes of rain, oblique and intermittent, but growing thicker and heavier. By the time she got to her stop the rain covered the pavement with a liquid patina. When she got off the bus she regretted not having accepted Sarrina's offer of a lift all the way home.

Grazia ran across the small, square courtyard of her building, jumping over the puddles that had formed in the gravel, but by the time she got to the front door she was soaked through just the same. She ran up the steps and pressed against the wet wood doors while searching for her keys in her jeans' pocket. The rain dripped annoyingly down her collar and against her neck.

In the foyer she unzipped her jacket, sighed, pulled her wet hair back off her face and wiped away the drops of rain. "Simone, I'm home!" she called out as she opened the door of her apartment, glancing back quickly over her shoulder. She heard a noise.

She saw him out of the corner of her eye. She knew instinctively it was him, even though he looked like someone else.

She had time only to take one step into the house, to turn slightly away and to say "No! No!" before Pit Bull aimed the silencer of a .22 towards her temple and pulled the trigger.

"Dottore? It's Matera. Sorry to disturb you but something has happened. Negro's boyfriend called. Something bad has happened . . ."

"WHERE AM I?"

"Nowhere."

He couldn't give her an answer. He could have said Imola, but it wasn't true because they were almost in Castel San Pietro. If she were to ask him again a little bit later he would have said Bologna. They weren't anywhere. They were on the motorway.

The girl moved around on the bed behind him. He looked at her in the rear-view mirror that he had modified so that he could see over the divider that separated the driving cabin from the living space of the camper van. He wanted to keep an eye on her, but couldn't do it while he was driving. Nor could he turn around. On the motorway everything is in front of you.

The girl tried to get up, but she was only able to turn onto her side. Her arms were locked behind her back with a pair of handcuffs and her ankles were tied with a rope that was also tied to her wrists. *Incaprettata* was the technical term for it, goat-tied, or practically, since for a full goat-tie he should have also tied the rope around her neck. He watched her in the rear-view mirror as if on a small monitor. She was trying to keep her head up and kept whimpering and mumbling. It sounded like she wasn't fully conscious. She let herself go, her neck flopped over her shoulder, her head lolled off the pillow, her eyes were shut.

She groaned.

"Stay still Ispettore. As soon as I can stop I'll come and check on you."

He stopped beneath an overpass to look at her. He didn't like stopping there – the police could come and start asking questions. On the motorway, life is movement. If you stop, it's because you need help.

He got out of the driver's seat and ran to the sliding door, shutting the driver's door behind him. It was raining really hard. In three short metres he got soaked; the drops fell with such force that it seemed to be raining even below the shelter of the overpass.

"Let's see."

He turned the girl over onto her stomach and ran a hand through her hair, pushing it off her temples. She groaned faintly as if she didn't want to wake up. She was all right: there was nothing wrong with her. She had a bluish bump on her temple, a cut and a patch of hair covered with sticky blood. He had shot at her with a plastic bullet that had a minimal amount of powder in it. He had wanted only to stun her, not to kill her.

He turned her over onto her side, pulled her arms out from underneath her hips and then raised her head and rested it on the pillow. When he looked down he realised that her eyes were open. She might have blurred vision, but even so she stared at him from under the hair that had fallen over her face.

"Are you Pit Bull?"

"Yes."

"Why did you kidnap me? What are you going to do to me?"

"Nothing. For now, anyway."

He left her side and ran back around to the driver's cab, getting soaked again. The rain came crashing down on the tarmac. Vittorio had to open his window and lean out into the rain to look behind and make sure no cars were coming. He crept forward slowly to get back into the traffic.

WHEN PIT BULL OPENED THE DOOR OF THE CAMPER
van for the second time, Grazia was awake and fully conscious.
Her whole body ached as if she had flu. The light and cool air
made her move and groan in pain; she had tugged on the
handcuffs and now her wrists hurt.

Pit Bull had a real face. It was identical to the one in the
photographs – he had a straight nose, regular features and short
hair. His thoughts didn't show through his serious expression.
And, as in the photographs, his expression seemed flat, rather
than mysterious. Maybe it was because he was used to wearing so
many different masks and dressing up to become other people.
But like this, naked, without a mask, he was no longer anything,
he was anonymous. Only his eyes said something about him. His
eyes were those of the child in the photograph: green, calm,
neither melancholy nor enthusiastic, simply cautious, as if he was
waiting. They were not the eyes of a killer.

Grazia was scared. She was alone, unarmed and tied up. Pit Bull
stood over her.

"What do you want?" she asked. "Why did you bring me here?
What are you going to do to me?"

Pit Bull had a Glock with a silencer tucked into the belt of his
trousers. Grazia gasped when he took it out. She tugged on the
handcuffs. They burned her wrists all the way up to her elbow. He
held the gun without gripping it; he just held it gently in his hand,

as if to show her. A short automatic; it was compact and square.

"First I shot you with a reduced .22. This is a .40 calibre pistol, with a full load and with a hollow tip. With one of these I can blow your head off Ispettore. Am I clear?" Grazia didn't reply. She just lay there with her eyes wide open, her mouth agape and her breath held in. "Am I clear?" he repeated.

Grazia nodded. She looked at him coming towards her and turned away when he pulled a stiletto knife out of his pocket.

"I took you because it was easier," he said, while cutting through the cord that held her ankles. Then he unlocked the handcuffs. "I watched you when you went into my house. And when you came out of the Questura. You were the only woman on the team."

"What are you going to do with me?"

She didn't expect an answer, and he didn't give one. She got up from the bed slowly, like a convalescent, first sitting up and then getting slowly to her feet, hunched over so as not to hit her head on the ceiling of the van.

"Wait! Wait!" she said. She felt pins and needles in her calves and thighs, all the way up to her bum. Her knees buckled. She would have fallen back down onto the bed if he hadn't held her up and helped her take the first step.

When they reached the door Grazia felt scared. He's going to kill me now, she thought. He's going to take me into a field and make me get on my knees and shoot me. She imagined herself like one of the many photographs of dead people that she had seen: damp, covered with mud, open-mouthed.

"Careful," he said, placing a hand over her head so she wouldn't bump it as she stepped outside. She flinched and resisted, though with some uncertainty.

"It's useless. You know that, don't you?" she blurted out, too quickly to make it seem like a threat. "It's only a question of time. Sooner or later they'll get you."

He stepped out of the van and pulled her down after him, holding her by the hand as if she were a child. Straightaway she stepped in a puddle. There was a little wooden house, not much bigger than a hut, with the door open. Behind it a grassy path led up the hill towards a clearing and then into the woods. Beyond the woods she could see a way over from the motorway. It was far away but close enough for her to hear the sound of lorries passing in the distance. It felt like they were in the mountains.

"Over there," Pit Bull said, tipping his head towards the hut. "And don't worry Ispettore. I am not going to kill you."

Inside it was almost warm. Almost. It was damp, but a cool kind of damp, as if the house had been closed for a long time. It wasn't cold because an electric heater was plugged in. The heating element wasn't enough to heat the room, but it made things somewhat more bearable. There was a chimney, too, and a bundle of wood lay ready to be burnt on top of some crumpled newspaper, but it hadn't been lit. Grazia shrugged, rubbing her arms. Her bomber jacket was still in the camper van; she was only wearing jeans and a T-shirt.

"Where are we?"

"In the Tusco-Emilian Apennines. Between Bologna and Firenze, on the downward slopes."

"They'll find you. It's not a very good place to hide."

"It doesn't matter. I only need a couple of days."

"They'll find you sooner than that. I know what's going to happen. The carabinieri know the place, they'll get the signal and they'll come and investigate."

Pit Bull looked at her. It seemed to Grazia that he smiled a little. But maybe it was more of an ironic expression of smug self-satisfaction than a smile, like the expression he wore in the photograph, as a child.

"No, your people are already looking for you. But somewhere else."

Grazia furrowed her brow and squinted at Pit Bull. He was smiling more openly now. Why were they looking for her somewhere else?

"I left your mobile phone at a motorway service station and switched it to silent so that no-one would hear it ring."

Grazia felt a wave of despair rush over her. The police would have found the mobile thanks to the radio transmitter, pin-pointed the location it was coming from and searched the entire area. At least for a couple of days. She couldn't count on them. She couldn't count on any one any more. It was just the two of them: her and him. Her and Pit Bull.

Through her despair she suddenly felt a burst of strong, solid anger that made her clench her fists with rage. She wanted to throw herself on him and that expressionless, serious, careful gaze of his. She wanted to punch him, kick him, choke him. He seemed to guess what she was thinking because he took a step back and pulled the gun with the silencer out of his waistband.

"Don't do it," he said. "You might be faster than me. Maybe you're even stronger. You probably even know martial arts. I've never punched anyone, not even when I was a child. But I don't need to. I shoot."

He raised his arm and pointed the gun at Grazia, who retreated into herself, like a turtle, and turned away, covering her face with her hands. When she lowered them, letting them fall to her sides, Pit Bull had already put the gun away.

"I don't know martial arts," Grazia said. "Sometimes I have to beat people up, but usually I just catch them. Can I have my jacket? I'm cold with only this T-shirt on."

SHE SEEMED CALMER NOW, AS IF SHE FINALLY UNDER-
stood that he had no intention of killing her. Not immediately
anyway. She used her bomber jacket like a blanket; she had taken
off her jeans and her socks and hung them in front of the heater
to dry. It wasn't so cold any more, but nevertheless she huddled
under the jacket because she didn't want him to see her legs. He
had already checked them out. She wasn't bad looking. Not bad at
all, he thought.

They ate sandwiches from a bag that he had bought at the
Pavesi service station at the entrance to the Bologna–Firenze
motorway. They drank Coke from the can and sat on the
carpet in front of the fireplace. At one point she shivered,
exaggeratedly.

"Brrr. Look at all that wood. Why don't we light a fire?"

He didn't even answer. She knew he wasn't stupid enough to
attract attention with a plume of smoke coming from an old villa.

"Where are the owners? Did you kill them?"

"No. They only come here at the weekends. I don't kill unless I
have to."

"How many people have you killed?"

He didn't need to calculate to tell her. He remembered them:
every one. He could see their deaths taking place in front of him,
like movies that he could rewind and see where he had made
mistakes. All his killings were calculable in ghostly bank transfers

on numbered accounts. Everything had been taken into consideration, down to the smallest detail.

"Eighteen? Twenty? Twenty-five?"

"Fifty-nine."

"Shit."

He had taken the magazines from the .22 and from Grazia's Beretta and put them in his pocket. He had taken the silencer off the Glock and placed the gun on the carpet, next to his leg. It was already loaded with a bullet, all he needed to do was remove the safety with a flick of his thumb, press the trigger and shoot.

He watched as she leaned forward on her hands and knees to get another sandwich from the bag. Chicken and rocket, no. Hardboiled egg and tuna, no. Peppers and prosciutto, yes. Then she sat back down and pulled her bomber jacket up over her. Only the tips of her toes, which she was wiggling together, and the tent made by her knees were visible.

"There've been some Mafia killers who have killed more people than that: Brusca, Aglieri, Spatuzza . . . When I was in Palermo there was a guy who had killed almost two hundred people."

Was she trying to provoke him? Did she want to see him react? He had no reactions. He did things differently to those other men. He told her so.

"I do something different."

"I know. You're a professional. You're Pit Bull."

Did she want to get him to talk? She looked at him per-severingly. She had crumbs around her mouth and kept one arm underneath her jacket, tugging at her big toe. What was she trying to do? Make him lose his patience? Trick him?

"You study all the details, you dress up, you fabricate your own weapons . . . who taught you everything? Don Masino?"

"No. He taught me how to kill. I took classes for the rest: acting, speech, make-up. I did an apprenticeship at an armoury. I worked with a mechanic. I almost completed a degree in computers, chemistry and nursing. I studied only what I needed to know and then I stopped."

"You're very patient . . ."

"It's my job."

"You spent a lot of time . . ."

"I have a lot of time. I always did. This is what I have been doing since I was ten."

He looked up and realised she was staring at him. She was studying his face, as if she was looking for something. She had an expression that he couldn't quite understand, a little sad and a little tough. He got to his feet. It was dark outside. He turned on the bedside lamp but it wasn't bright enough to illuminate the room. He checked to see that the shutters were closed, then he lit a kerosene lamp and moved it closer to Grazia, who tipped her head to one side and shielded her face with her hand.

"I'm sorry, but I have to be able to see you Ispettore."

"Listen, do me a favour. Stop being so formal. It pisses me off. Do you want to maintain your distance so that it will be easier for you to kill me?"

"No. Why?"

"Well stop all this 'Ispettore' crap then, I'm here, I'm half naked, I'm your hostage and sooner or later you'll shoot me in the head. You can ditch the formalities, for Chrissakes."

He nodded. There was a rocking chair in the corner and he went and sat on it, disappearing into the shadows. The room wasn't big, but from where she was she could no longer see him. His voice seemed to come from the shadows. Sentences came out of the silence and hung suspended in the darkness. But he was able to see her. He saw her bra strap slipping off her shoulder, below her T-shirt sleeve; he saw how she had pulled back her hair and held it together with a stick of wood from the fireplace; he saw the curve of her chin when she bit her lip. Suddenly she was frightened.

"Can I ask you a question now?"

He didn't want to distract her, but there really was something he wanted to know. It had come to his mind when she had asked about his training.

"How did you know about Don Masino?"

"A man you tried to kill led us to him. He was practically dead, his arms and legs had been burnt off, but he managed to speak just the same."

"Oh."

"Did you kill Don Masino?"

"Yes."

"Why?"

"I was in danger. I killed everyone who could connect Vittorio Marchini to Pit Bull. But now even the dead can talk!"

It was only a joke, but she took it seriously. He watched as she leaned forward and peered into the darkness, trying to see his face.

"Give up. Collaborate with us. You can talk."

"Oh, please."

"You have so many things you could tell the judges: the killings, the names of the people you worked for, come on Vitto'! Brusca and the others all made it, you would too."

"Oh, please."

It was the first time she had called him by his name, and she had abbreviated it to make him feel at ease, but his instinct was to touch his gun. She must have guessed it because she shut up. She sat up on her knees, the bomber jacket falling to one side.

"By now everyone knows that Pit Bull exists; in a few days it'll be in the papers and everyone will know what you've done. You've come out of your silence, Vitto', you got what you wanted. Why do you need to kill me too?"

What was she saying? He didn't understand. What silence was she talking about? She was moving closer to him even though he had raised the gun in the dark. She kept one hand on the rug to keep her balance. He didn't want her to come any closer. He didn't want to shoot her just yet. So he said something, just to stop her.

"I don't know. Maybe."

She stopped. She sat back down on her heels. She looked at him attentively, uncertainly and, even though she still had her eye on the gun, she seemed less afraid. Better that way. He got up from his chair.

"That's enough. Now I want to sleep."

He pulled the handcuffs out of his pocket and came up to her. She hesitated for a moment and then turned around and offered her wrists to him. He eyed at her suspiciously as he grabbed first one wrist and then the other. Even if she was afraid of the gun she seemed quieter now. Better that way.

What silence was she talking about?

THEY SLEPT ON THE FLOOR, IN FRONT OF THE COLD fireplace, on mattresses he had pulled out of the bedroom. They couldn't sleep in the bedroom because there was only an old ceramic stove in there, and they couldn't light it because of the smoke. If her wrists hadn't been in handcuffs, Grazia would have hugged her knees and curled up in a ball. She was cold. Not because of the temperature in the room so much as because of the draughts. It had started raining again outside and an icy wind blew across the ground. The floor seemed to take away all their heat. She began to sniffle.

"What's the matter?" he asked. He was close to her shoulder. From his voice it sounded like he must have raised himself up on one elbow. Or else he was sitting up. "Can't you sleep?"

"I'm cold."

"I can hug you."

He moved closer to her. She held her breath, clenching her teeth. She tried not to stiffen when she felt his body next to hers under the blanket, when she felt him drape one arm over her shoulder and across her neck. She didn't want to make him angry, not after she had suggested he give himself up. She wanted to keep him as placid as possible. She felt his warm breath on her neck, his chest against her shoulders, his legs bent underneath hers. The thought occurred to her that if he hadn't been Pit Bull, if he hadn't killed 59 people, if she hadn't had her arms tied behind her back it would have been nice to fall asleep like that, sleepy and close to someone on a cold rainy night.

"No," he said, moving away from her. "It's no good. I'm cold too."

"Let's go in the bedroom. We'll bring the heater with us."

"No, the only socket is out here."

"Then let's bring the bed frames out here. That way we won't be on the ground."

"I don't think they'd fit through the door. We'd have to take them apart . . ."

Grazia looked over her shoulder and saw that he was sitting up. How absurd it was, she thought, the policeman and the assassin trying to get to sleep, as if on a camping trip. Let's all sleep in one room, come on.

"Come with me."

He helped her get to her feet. Grazia started to move towards the bedroom, but he stopped her and directed her towards the door. She resisted, instinctively.

"Let's go to the camper van," he said. "There's only one bed, but there are fewer draughts."

He put the cover over her head and pulled her outside, making her run barefoot across the wet gravel. Even though it took him barely a second to open the door of the camper and let her in, by the time he closed the door they were both soaked again.

"Shit," Grazia said. "What lousy weather."

"Turn around," he said, with his gun in his hand. Grazia stiffened for a second but did it anyway. She was surprised when she felt him undo the handcuffs.

"Take off your shirt."

"Why?" she asked, defensively.

"Because it's wet," he said, beginning to take off his clothes. Grazia pulled her T-shirt over her head. It was soaked through and it stuck to her skin. She was left in only her underwear. She hugged herself, shivering.

"Please," she said, "Let me keep my arms in front of me. Don't lock my hands behind me. I promise I won't do anything. I won't run away. Where would I go?"

He looked at her searchingly and then nodded. He made a gesture for her to extend her arms in front of her and locked the cuffs around her wrists. She murmured "thank you" and lay down on the bed. She pressed her back up against the wall and shut her eyes to avoid looking at him. He rested the gun on the floor and lay down next to her.

"Raise your arms," he said, but she didn't do it. She didn't understand. She looked at him in surprise, bent her elbows and with great difficulty raised her arms above her head. He took hold of the handcuffs, ducked underneath them and then made her lower her arms around him so they encircled his waist. Now her arms were blocked tight. She couldn't do anything. She couldn't get away without waking him. Or lean over and get his gun. Hit him. Strangle him with the cuffs.

"All right," he said. "Let's get some sleep."

Grazia closed her eyes. Outside, the rain was falling heavily on the metal roof of the camper van. It hit against the plexiglass of the window. It was falling hard. She liked the sound. It was warm inside the camper. The two of them were so close that they didn't even need the blanket.

She knew she wouldn't be able to sleep. She felt uncomfortable. She would have been uncomfortable with anyone except Simone. She had never felt comfortable with any of the men she had been with except for him. But it was different with Vittorio. Hugging him tight, her legs pressed against his, their faces very close, she felt the warmth of his skin. He was damp with perspiration. She felt his breath on her forehead. Holy Madonna, what a story, she thought. First I hunt down the fugitives, I study them as if they were my lovers and then climb into bed with them.

He couldn't sleep either. Grazia could tell from the way he tried not to move and the way he was breathing regularly. His left hand was under the pillow that she was resting her head on. It must have been uncomfortable for him, but he didn't move. His other hand was underneath him, resting on top of her elbow, his hand almost touching her stomach. Each time Grazia took a breath his fingers brushed her belly. She didn't move. She stayed still. Even though it was uncomfortable. She wished she could stretch out and relax the muscles in her legs. She could hear her heart beating in her ear pressed against the pillow, a pulsing beat, amplified. Very slowly she tried to move her head back. Then she opened her eyes and realised he was looking at her.

No, she thought, when she saw him move towards her. No, when he pushed her back on a shoulder, rolling her onto her back. No. Please, no.

He stared into her eyes. His face was expressionless, as blank as in those photographs, there was only that flat, green, expressionless gaze. He moved on top of her. She couldn't do anything to resist because her arms were locked around him. It was as if she were hugging him. She couldn't push him away and she wouldn't have done it anyway because she was scared. She was scared he would kill her, that he would get angry, that he would stick the gun in her mouth and blow her head off right there, on the bed. She was scared she would ruin everything, that she would lose that small advantage she had gained, that little window she had opened up inside him and that was the only thing that might save her life.

She closed her eyes when he pulled down her panties. She clenched her teeth and fists when he separated her legs. If her hands had been free she would have grabbed at the sheet. Instead she was forced to drape her arms around him as if she wanted it.

She couldn't do anything. She was scared of dying. She was scared of that feeling in her stomach that was growing stronger and stronger. It was a feeling that raised her up, that kept her suspended, that made her feel as if her body wasn't her own.

She felt him relax and slide onto his side, out of breath. She opened her eyes and saw that his were closed. He wasn't looking at her any more. She wondered what he was thinking; there was definitely something behind those blank eyes. She felt sticky, numb and dirty. She pulled away from him as far as she could.

She wanted to stay alive, she told herself. She wanted to get out of there, run away, go home to Simone. She wanted to arrest Pit Bull, take him in to the Questura. She wanted to shoot him, kill him, choke him with both hands. She wanted to shut her eyes and sleep.

It had been like looking at photographs of dead, naked people, she said to herself.

Another unpleasant experience to which her job had exposed her, and one from which she must remain detached.

"WHO'S GETTING THE RUSTICHELLA?"

Vittorio waved his receipt in the air carefully so his wallet wouldn't fall out from under his arm. He handed the receipt to the barman who tore it in half before handing it back.

"Do you want your coffee now? Or would you rather wait?"

"I'll wait."

He grabbed a few more napkins because the Rustichella was piping hot and he rested it on the round, mushroom-shaped table. He bit off a corner of his hot mozzarella sandwich and looked at the camper van, which was parked directly in front of the café. He realised he was still holding his wallet under his arm so he rested it on the table, moving aside the plates and the napkins stained with red tomato sauce from Spizzico.

He looked around the room for the man he had seen drive into the car park. He had watched each new car that arrived. He was looking for a man, a man on his own. No families, no couples, no women. But it couldn't be just any man. A boy in a black T-shirt, tall, "natural born killer" tattooed on his right bicep: no. A short man: no. A 25-year-old man with glasses and pimples: maybe. He left a dog in the car: no. A man about 40, with a moustache, long hair and a white "Oktoberfest" T-shirt, army trousers and black shoes: yes. He was carrying a coat over his arm, an orange motorway-maintenance-worker's coat lined with white and yellow and with ANAS printed across it: no. A man of about 30 with a yellow jumper, a blue shirt, open at the neck to show a white vest underneath, boots and jeans: yes. He comes into the café and orders a Rustichella, a can of Coke, a coffee and a scratch card: yes! Vittorio went back outside, started the engine and parked the camper van behind the man's Fiat Punto.

He took another bite of his sandwich. It was already getting cold. The first corner had been hot, the middle of the sandwich was empty and cold, and the end, where the mozzarella and tomato had been, was still frozen. The man ate much slower than he did. He had only just started his Rustichella and he hadn't yet poured his Coke, so Vittorio took a coin out of his wallet and scratched away at the LOTTO card he had bought. He won another one, but he folded the card in half and dropped it on top of the pile of empty plates.

"Ready for your espresso?"

Vittorio nodded, dropping the last piece of the Rustichella in the rubbish. While he was finishing his Coke two agents from the motorway patrol came in. They leaned on the counter right in front of him and looked around at the customers before placing their own order. They looked at him and saw a man drinking a Coke, wearing overalls and clogs, with big ears, a little bit of red beard. And then they turned their back on him.

"Excuse me."

Vittorio stepped between them to get his coffee. He took it back to his table and blew on it before taking a sip. He looked at the man with the yellow jumper and realised that he had finished; he was scraping the sugar out of the bottom of his cup. And the LOTTO card was no longer there. So Vittorio tucked his wallet under his arm and followed the man out. He stopped for a minute in the doorway, opening the door for the agents, giving them a cordial smile; thank goodness for the keepers of the law. Then he hurried to catch up with the man, who was already climbing into his car and looking around: what the hell? whose camper van is this . . . ?

"Here I come, here I am, sorry."

But instead of going to the camper, Vittorio went up to the man, who was getting into his car, took out his .22, aimed the silencer at the man's temple and pulled the trigger.

GRAZIA TENSED HER SHOULDERS AND THEN RELAXED
them, contracting the muscles in her neck and tipping her head
back as far as possible. She needed to cough, but tried to stay still,
because with every movement the cord tightened around her
throat a little bit more. This time he had tied her in a full goat-tie,
with the rope going around her neck, down her back, around her
wrists and all the way down to her ankles. Grazia gripped her
sports socks; her back was arched like a gondola. The muscles in
her legs burned. She would have managed pretty well if it hadn't
been for the coughing that intermittently forced her to move, and
that made the rope tighten. Now she needed to cough again.

She contracted the muscles in her stomach and opened her
mouth wide, trying to keep her throat still. But the desire to cough
made her chest swell. She stuck her tongue out when the cord
pulled a little tighter round her windpipe, and when she tried to
take a quick breath, oh god, oh god, she moved, her foot slipped
out of her grasp and the rope pulled tight. The terror made her
eyes pop wide open. She lost control of her muscles and tried to
grab her foot again, clawing at the air with the fingers of her free
hand, spitting out a choked growl that made her tongue scrape
against her teeth.

That's the way Vittorio found her when he came back to the
camper van. She was choking, the veins on her temples were
swollen, tears were streaming out of the corners of her eyes and a

dribble of bloody spittle ran down the pillow. He jumped into the van and grabbed her ankles with one hand while reaching for his stiletto with the other. He freed her wrists and tried to raise her up, but she pushed him away and fell back down onto the bed, her knees collapsing into her chest, gasping for breath, retching emptily.

"I'm sorry," he said. "I thought you'd stay still."

"Fuck you!" she growled. She put a hand to her mouth. Her scraped tongue hurt. "You don't give a shit!" she said, coughing into her hands and trying to round out her words as if she had a sweet in her mouth. "You're going to kill me anyway!"

Vittorio shrugged. He put the stiletto back in his pocket and grabbed her by the arm, forcing her to get up out of the van and walk barefoot across the wet gravel. He pushed her into the villa and pulled the Glock out of the holster on his belt, waiting for her reaction.

"Who is that? What did you do to him?"

Sitting on the rocking chair in front of the fireplace was a man with a yellow jumper. He was tied to the chair and had a rag in his mouth. His eyes were closed and there was dried blood in his hairline. The tips of his fingers were blackened, as if they had been burnt. On the table next to the chair was Grazia's gun. Vittorio picked it up. He checked to make sure it was loaded.

"What are you going to do?" Grazia asked.

"I want to die."

"What are you going to do?" she asked again, because she didn't understand what he meant. He slid the barrel back, making a bullet drop into it. He walked up behind Grazia and pushed the barrel of the Glock into her side, hard, hurting her. He took advantage of her surprise to force the Beretta into her hand, wrapping his fingers around hers. He pressed his chest into her back, and locked his left arm around her and pointed the Glock into her chin. Then he pushed her towards the man in the chair, propping her up when she slipped back on the floor because of her wet socks. He pointed the Beretta straight at the man's face.

"Why?" Grazia yelled. "Why me? Why?"

But she knew why: because if she had shot him they would have believed it. They would have looked at the gun in her hand and seen that she had killed that faceless man, whom they would assume to be Pit Bull. Naturally, after having shot him, she too would die.

She began to understand. This was no plea for help. Vittorio had begun to sign his killings in order to prepare the way for his escape. To kill himself, Pit Bull first had to exist. She still didn't know why he did it – whether because he had no other choice or because he was still, at heart, a child – she didn't know and she no longer cared. In a few minutes she would have shot an innocent man and then she too would be dead.

"No!" Grazia said, trying to resist, "Wait! Wait wait wait!" She planted her feet on the floor, pushing back against him, but she slipped and lost her footing, her chin falling directly onto Vittorio's gun, her head pressed against his chest. She realised Vittorio's hand was on the bridge of the Beretta too, and his finger pressed down tightly on hers inside the metal eye. She tried to shut her eyes, because she couldn't lower her head.

"No! she screamed. "No! No!"

She couldn't take it any more; his finger curled over hers.

A round of gunshot exploded from the Beretta into the man's chest, digging a row of holes into him on the left side of his body and up to his shoulder. Vittorio corrected the hold and planted another three bullets in his face. The man fell over, first swelling like a sail and grabbing the arms of the chair until one of them broke off, then he flopped down. He might have yelled, but any sound was lost in the wild, never-ending noise of gunfire.

Vittorio loosened his hold on the gun and Grazia's hand slipped out, leaving the gun in his hand. She fell to her knees, panting for breath. She needed to scream. She took deep gulps of air as if struck by an asthma attack.

Vittorio went up to the man to make sure his face was no longer there. He had the two guns in his hand, the Glock in his left – which he held by the bridge, like a stone – and the Beretta in the right – ready to shoot again. He glanced quickly at Grazia, who was now kneeling on the ground, both hands on the floor, struggling to breathe and making deep retching sounds. He leaned over the chair to look at the man.

In that very moment Grazia found her breath. The yell inside her came out with so much force that she scraped her tongue again. She howled as she scratched at the floor with her nails and pressed her feet into the carpet. Her wet socks got hold of the ground and Grazia pounced, fast and compact, like a tiger, towards Pit Bull.

THOUGHT: A BULLET IN THE STOMACH.

With a bullet in the stomach Grazia would certainly have died and yet would plausibly have had time to shoot the man.

Pit Bull was leaning over the now faceless man. He didn't need to shoot him any more. He was thinking about a bullet in the stomach, when suddenly he heard Grazia's yell and perceived her movements. He knew he wouldn't have had time to move – like when you hear a gun shot, it's already too late. He didn't even have the time to turn around and raise his gun when she rammed into him. So, it was true that she was faster and stronger, because she knocked him backwards with such force he almost lifted off the floor. He flew against the wall and hit the back of his head with a thud that reverberated through his teeth, stunning him for an instant, but only an instant. He didn't fall down. When he gathered himself, he raised his right arm and fired the Beretta, because the Glock, which he had been holding on to like a rock in his left hand, was no longer there. One shot, one instinct. He didn't need to aim because Grazia was so near.

He would have got her if she hadn't slipped.

GRAZIA FELT THE BULLET BURN PAST HER EAR AND hit the wall behind her. She fell to the floor. She felt the ridged plastic handle of Vittorio's gun. She grabbed it and fired without even looking, even at the risk of shooting herself, because she was still falling. She didn't hit him, but forced him off to the side; he covered his face with his hands because splinters of wood came flying off the wall and tore into his cheek. This gave her room to move, jump into position and run towards the open door of the villa. Vittorio fired another shot at her, but he missed because he was still blinded by the wooden splinters.

She ran outside as fast as she could, slamming her hand into the camper van and then sliding around it to the other side, pressing up against its edge to hide. She realised it had started raining again; she had to narrow her eyes to see through the heavy drops.

Her socks were soaked through; they weighed heavily around her ankles. She yanked them off and threw them far away. The cold ground underfoot reminded her that Pit Bull could shoot at her legs from under the camper so she moved behind the tyre to gain cover. She stood with her back to the van, her feet together, her arms raised. She held the gun with both hands and kept it pressed against her face for protection, as if it were a pillow on a thundery night. It occurred to her that she didn't even know how many bullets were left. It also occurred to her that she was dealing with a professional killer who'd shot 59 people. Now 60. On the other side of that metal wall of the camper was Pit Bull. He wanted to kill her. She was alone. No-one could help her. Her eyes welled with tears. She tried to hold them back with a frown and let out a long, desperate groan. She would have covered her face with her hands, but she was afraid of being found like that, defenceless and blind. That fear forced her to open her eyes and hold back her tears with a series of short, wet gulps of air, the way a child does. She breathed in deeply through her nose, inhaling a mixture of salty tears and cold rain, and glanced around the corner of the camper, then retreated with such speed that she bumped her head on it.

He hadn't seen her.

She moved into a crushing wall of rain, leaning slightly forwards, her legs flexed, her elbows bent into the sides of her stomach to balance the gun. In a moment he'd be there. She could either run away (and get shot in the back), go out (and get shot in the face), or wait and do nothing. No matter what, she would die. So she squeezed the gun, screamed "fuck you" and threw herself around the corner of the camper.

THOUGHT: I CAN'T SHOOT HER WITH THIS.

He couldn't shoot her with the Beretta. He couldn't shoot her with the same 9×21 bullets with which he shot "Pit Bull". His whole plan would go up in smoke. He had the wrong gun in his hand.

He would have shot her anyway, because she was armed, but when Grazia jumped out from behind the camper he was busy thinking: I can't shoot her with this gun. It was the first time he had ever had a thought *during* one of his manoeuvres. He pressed the trigger with only a fraction of a second's delay, but when he was thrown backwards he realised that his delay was fatal, she had shot him first.

His shoulder slammed against the wall of the villa. Suddenly, with an oppressive feeling in his chest that was neither bothersome nor painful, only a tightness at the level of his heart, he felt a great sense of silence. He had never felt such silence. It was as if his ears were full of cotton wool; he couldn't hear the buzz in his head or the thick whistle in his ears. It was a silence that wrapped up everything. It rolled down through him and filled him up entirely. It was total silence.

A part of him thought: the shot that killed a man. A part of him thought: after being shot in the heart you survive for ten seconds, but in fact you're already dead.

1) The anaesthetising effect of the adrenaline suddenly passed,

leaving him with a lacerating, burning feeling which made him hug his arms to his chest and squeeze his eyes shut. A part of him thought: no.

2) The internal haemorrhage lowered his blood pressure suddenly, making him fall to his knees on the wet grass. He brought his hands to his chest. A part of him was able to feel the warm flow that soaked his shirt. It ran through his fingers. Thought: Mamma.

3) He fell back on his heels, lost his centre of balance and fell. He tried to yell, but only a deep, guttural gurgle came out. A part of him thought: no, now I'll get up.

4) A contraction in his heart. The cavernous emptiness: immobile, impenetrable, deaf, total.

5) Only pain, no thoughts, no movements. Just pain. Strong, acute, pungent pain. Nothing else.

6) Another dip in his blood pressure; his back muscles relaxed and his head tipped forward. His arms flopped down by his sides; the backs of his hands hit the grass.

7) Less energy with which to feel the pain. The icy rain on the back of his neck awakens his consciousness. A part of him thinks: how can I who am I what am I thinking what am I feeling how can I.

8) His head falls forward. His mouth opens. He was thinking.

9) His head droops further still, it touches the wet grass. Thought: too bad.

10) His forehead touches the ground. He disappears into a fuzzy whiteness as if he were diving into an ocean of grass. Thought: it's over. Thought: really. Thought: now.

"YOU KNOW, NEGRO, YOU'RE THE ONLY POLICE OFFICER I know who, in an armed conflict, has run a greater risk of death from catching pneumonia than from taking a bullet."

"If you tease her you'll make her angry, Sarrina. In a little while she'll be your boss and then you'll have a problem. What are they going to do with you, Grazia? Are they going to promote you?"

"I don't know . . ."

"Of course they are. Armed conflict with a dangerous criminal . . . I think you'll be exempted from service. Christ, you were even wounded."

"Matera, it's a plaster . . ."

"How can they make her a direttore when she's got no degree?"

"Get a degree and have them make you commissario."

"I'm no good at school."

"So get them to give you a good position. Go back to Palermo, to the Antimafia . . . no, to SCICO, the Head Office for Investigations into organised crime. Get them to give you a position where you can move up the ladder."

"She's not going to leave Bologna, she can't. She's pregnant."

"Is that true? Grazia, is that true?"

"I don't know."

"Did you take the test?"

"I think she did. I think she's pregnant."

*

She hadn't done the test. There hadn't been time. It was still in her jacket pocket. When she managed to stop screaming she fell to her knees. It had taken her a long time to get her thoughts together. She went into the camper van and tried to call for help on the CB radio, but it didn't work because of the mountains. Her next thought was that she would have to turn Vittorio over and search for his keys.

It was a group of policemen from Roncobilaccio that eventually found her: a soaking, barefoot girl said she was a police detective and that she had killed a pit bull. They took her to casualty and then Sarrina and Matera showed up. Carlisi wanted to see her at the Mobile Unit immediately so that he could find out what went on before the Questore, the magistrate and the journalists arrived on the scene. The report will get done tomorrow, for goodness sake, with all that you've been through. The story wasn't complicated. He had kidnapped her so that his death would seem credible. She managed to get free and shoot him before he shot her, though she still didn't know how. The psychologist and the others hadn't understood a thing about Pit Bull. It had nothing to do with silence. He wanted to get back inside the silence, but in another way. He wanted to keep going. Maybe he liked it; maybe he simply didn't know how to do anything else. She didn't care. It wasn't her job to understand him. She had caught him.

This time she accepted the lift all the way home. Sarrina even drove into the courtyard and Matera opened the car door for her.

"Are you all right, getting out by yourself?"

"For Chrissakes."

"Okay, but watch yourself. And let us know – if you're pregnant, I mean."

She climbed the stairs slowly because she ached everywhere. Even her tongue hurt. Her head was spinning. She thought about the rain, the camper van, Pit Bull. She bit her lip. No, she wouldn't say anything. Not now. Tomorrow.

Matera was right, she could get a good position somewhere and have a good career. And what if she was pregnant? What should she do, get married? And if she didn't want to keep it? And if she wanted to, what would she do? Would she lose everything? And Simone?

Grazia opened the door and saw Simone standing next to the sofa. He stood very still, pretending not to have heard her. He must have only just got home because he still had his coat on.

"Simone, I'm home . . ." she said.

"We need to talk."

UN GIORNO DOPO L'ALTRO . . . IL TEMPO SE NE VA . . . Le strade sono sempre uguali . . . le stesse case.

I opened my eyes and saw him standing there. He was reaching out a hand to wake me up; he thought I was asleep. But I'm not. I'm awake. I've fallen asleep a lot of times with the headphones on, but not while listening to Tenco. I couldn't.

Now, when I listen to his music, it doesn't have the same effect on me that it used to. Before, I couldn't listen to it without my throat closing up and tears coming to my eyes. My throat gets choked now too, but not for the same reason. Now it's because of a sense of suspense, waiting, anguish. It's fear. I don't know what will happen and I'm still not sure I made the right choice. I know things haven't got much better, but at least it's something, and with feelings, it's the nuances that count.

I open my eyes and take off my headphones, even if all I have to do is simply show my documents. I look at him from a distance while still floating along on Tenco's thick smoky voice. I know he'll say something to me. And I will have to answer him, even if everything is in order. Police are police, even in Switzerland.

Twelve and a half hours, with a change in Basel, and then the train goes directly on to Copenhagen. Five hundred forms for me to fill out and 397 for Dog, who has the right to a 40 per cent discount. Plus I have all his documents: the certificate that shows he's registered at the dog kennel, that he has a tattoo or microchip, that he had his anti-rabies shot more than 20 days ago but less than eleven months, not to mention the receipt for payment of 8670 lire. All this without knowing what Kristine will do when she sees me arrive with him. She might run up to me and kiss me like in an old Hollywood movie, or she might kick us both out. That's why I'm scared.

I could have flown to Copenhagen, but, besides the fact that it would have cost more, I would have had to send Dog through the cargo area like a package and put him in a cage, and I just couldn't do that. This way I can keep him on a lead. He only needs a muzzle. Putting it on him was easy. He didn't seem to mind.

The Swiss policeman takes my documents and studies them as if trying to memorise every detail, then he looks at Dog on the floor next to me and raises an eyebrow. I know what he's about to say. It's the reason I've been travelling in an empty compartment for the past three and a half hours. So I say it first.

"No, he's not a pit bull. He's a Staffordshire bull terrier. He looks like a pit bull, but he's not."